Steven Kincaid is the last unmarried male in his family . . . the much-lamented unmarried male. He knows he needs a good woman, but the right one hasn't come along in his thirty-seven years. Until his new neighbour moves in.

Meg is not the marrying kind, and Mr. Kincaid needs to keep his distance so that she can keep her sanity. Unfortunately, the accident-prone man is getting under her skin — and she is starting to like it. But growing up as she did has made her wary and feeling unworthy of love. When her parents show up, it will be up to Steven to be her buffer and the thorn in her side that makes her re-examine her life.

That Pushy Kincaid
Copyright © 2019 Quinn Clancy and Mary Clancy
ISBN: 978-1-4874-2221-9
Cover art by Martine Jardin

Published by eXtasy Books Inc or
Devine Destinies, an imprint of eXtasy Books Inc

Look for us online at:
www.eXtasybooks.com or www.devinedestinies.com

THAT PUSHY KINCAID
TRIPLE THREAT BOOK 3

BY

QUINN CLANCY AND MARY CLANCY

DEDICATION

This series is dedicated to our brothers, Raymond and Norm, as well as our father, Gerald. You are all dearly missed!

CHAPTER ONE

Steven Kincaid had grown to despise microwave dinners with a passion. Tough beef dinners, rubbery vegetable dinners, mushy pasta dinners. He hated them all. But still, he kept his freezer full of the little trays with their tasty little pictures, hoping one day he would peel back a label and discover that what was depicted on the packaging was really inside. It was an exercise in continuous disappointment.

Takeout food had its advantages. It was usually quite palatable, and he didn't have to do so much as push a button to get it. Well, he conceded, he did have to use the phone and fish money out of his pocket, but the end result was a darned sight more appealing than cardboard steak and lasagna that resembled wet tissue dipped in tomato soup.

He sighed hugely and gave his pseudo-mashed potato a dispirited shove around the tray. Such was the life of a confirmed, thirty-seven-year-old bachelor, he mused. Long evenings in a deathly quiet apartment with nothing but a television and paperwork for company. Well, it was almost quiet.

Another thump came from the apartment next door.

Steven's ear quirked automatically. For two days an odd assortment of people had been traipsing in and out of his new neighbor's place—men with long hair and bulging biceps, women with colorful clothes and dangling jewelry. He'd yet to lay eyes on the woman who was moving in, but he'd guess she was a hippie type if her friends were any indication.

The last tenant had been cheerful and minded his own

business, keeping to his side of the old renovated duplex with dependable consistency. Steven had never felt the need to purchase earplugs until now. Surely the woman next door could get settled without all that bumping and groaning.

He could have gone to his sisters' house across town for some company. However, the twins were always telling him he needed a woman, so that was out for now. Disagreeing was not an option. His brothers were all married with kids, and even his college buddies had taken the plunge this past year. It was assumed that he was next to go. The last man standing.

As the racket in the other apartment intensified, he shoved his hands through his sable-brown hair in frustration. Was there really any need? he wondered again. How could one person have so much *stuff* to move from one place to another?

A low moan reached him as he dumped the remains of his dinner, the sound making him think of sex and the fact that he hadn't had any in months. The last woman he'd dated had seen him as a convenient step up the corporate ladder, and he'd spotted the signs. He was definitely making it a rule from now on not to go out with business associates.

The phone whirred when he went back to the living room. Steven stared at it for a moment before picking up the receiver, contemplating the merits of a hot shower on his aching six-foot-three frame. It could be his mother calling from Bay de Chance to enquire about his love life. Perhaps it was his partner, Jonas Mackenzie, wanting to pick his brain over some computer program they were working on.

"Hello," he answered on the fourth ring, hoping the other half of MK Electronics was indeed calling to relieve his boredom.

"Is the noise bothering you?" asked a husky, feminine voice.

"Pardon?"

"The noise. Is it bothering you?"

Realizing it must be the new tenant, Steven sat up in his chair and decided to have a little fun at her expense. "Heck, I don't mind a bit of sound interrupting my sleep. My bird, on the other hand, is having a problem."

"Your bird?"

"My cockatoo. Bazil's very upset." Steven grinned and relaxed in his chair again.

Silence stretched for a minute.

"You have a . . . cockatoo . . . named Bazil." It was not a question, more like a slow statement spoken to a dim-witted child.

"Yes, and he's extremely agitated."

"How do you know?"

"Well," he postulated, trying to recall the condition of an abused bird he'd seen at the vet's clinic, "he keeps plucking his feather's out. It's a terrible sight. Poor Baz is just wretched."

A soft gasp echoed in his ear, and he congratulated himself on his meanness.

The woman tremulously remarked, "I am so very sorry. No more noise. I promise." She hung up.

Steven idly wondered how she'd got his number. Then again, the landlord was a gossip and tended to chat more than was tolerable. The elderly gent had probably dropped his name in conversation, and she'd looked it up in the phone book. How sweet of the lady to be concerned with his comfort — and he'd laid a guilt trip on her over a nonexistent bird. How shameful!

He chuckled dryly to himself. Old age must be creeping up on him if he found being cantankerous that amusing. At least the din next door had stopped.

The phone trilled again, cutting into his moment of

smugness. "Hello."

The Voice said, "I didn't think we were allowed to have pets here."

"Ah, no." That particular detail had escaped his lying brain. "Mr. Rupert doesn't know. Don't turn me in," he begged pitifully. "Baz doesn't have anyone else."

"Doesn't he squawk a lot?" she demanded suspiciously.

"He's much quieter than my new neighbor."

"I've apologized for that."

"It didn't help Baz. He's damned near plucked himself featherless! I'll have to put him on the Happy Pill all over again." By now, Steven was choking on his laughter and couldn't contain a snicker.

"Do you really have a cockatoo?" The Voice turned slightly menacing. "Because if you are so cruel and deranged as to deliberately yank my chain—"

"*Cruel?* You're the one giving me a headache!"

"I'm coming over to inspect your bird."

Alarmed, he bolted upright in his chair. "You can't."

"Why not?"

"He's ... uh ... pecked himself into exhaustion. Yeah, he's asleep."

"I don't believe you have a cockatoo," she stated firmly.

"I do. But thanks to the clamor coming from your place, he's not only pestered but frighteningly ugly."

"No living creature is ugly."

Uh-huh, she's a hippie all right. "Bazil's bald."

"Bald is *in.*" She slammed down the phone.

Steven held the receiver away from his ear and smirked. She may be a throwback to the *Me* generation but she had enough compassion to be influenced by the image of a tortured white parrot—whoever *she* was. He should have asked for a name. It was probably Moonbeam or Sunflower—Sunny for short.

The thumping began anew. Bump. Ping.

Ping? What the hell is she pinging?

Plainly, she'd figured there was no Baz and had gone back to her hullabaloo with a vengeance. It was his own fault, he knew, but that concession only aggravated him all the more. What had he done to deserve this torment? He was a good son, supportive brother, loyal friend. Hell, he'd even volunteered to coach a minor hockey league team.

There was a lull in the activity on the other side of the wall. Steven breathed a sigh of relief. The Voice must be finished for the night.

Tap . . . tap . . . tap.

He groaned. Maybe she wasn't finished.

It was just past eleven o'clock. Resigned to being subjected to the discordant sounds for a while longer, he rose and ambled to the den. Shutting the door resolutely, he turned his attention to the computer and struck a key to banish the screen saver. Calling up a file that listed his current investments and how each of them stood at the market day's end, he leaned back in his swivel chair and pondered what to do with the pile of money he'd hoarded in his savings account.

Soooo much to spend and nothing and no one to spend it on. Perhaps now was the time to start looking for a house. His apartment was modest and suited his bachelor lifestyle, but waiting for the right woman to come along was taking longer than he'd anticipated. He had put off searching for a place to really call home until he found The One, that special someone to share his life and a few kids with. So far, it hadn't happened.

His friends, Jonas—who'd married his cousin, Viv—and JJ, had offered to set him up. His sisters, Cass and Caro, were single but considered it far more important to see him married off than to do the deed themselves. Ma and Pop, who lived in Bay de Chance near his four younger brothers and their families, constantly reiterated their theory that there must be some available female in the St. John's area that he could find and charm into an engagement.

Yes, Steven mused, the world was full of matchmakers. None of them, however, were having any better luck at finding him a mate than he was.

The phone on the desk interrupted his meditation.

"How's Baz?" she sweetly enquired.

"Having seizures. Are you about done over there? Is it safe to retire in peace?" No matter how old or how funky the woman was, she did have a sexy voice.

"I'm afraid not." She exhaled loudly, communicating mock regret.

"If you're not done soon I'll complain to the landlord," he warned mildly. He was bluffing, of course. Didn't everyone make noise when shifting their belongings from one location to another? "What's your name, anyway?"

"Ezmerelda." The line went dead.

He grinned. She had a sense of humor. He frowned. Unless that really was her name. It was no worse than Moonbeam, was it?

Trudging through to his bedroom half an hour later, he'd all but put the faceless female out of his mind. He stripped down to his boxers and slid beneath the thick comforter on his king-size bed. Computers and software programs flitted through his head as he thought about another hectic day at the office. Grateful to feel his eyelids getting heavy, he surrendered to sleep when it came for him.

Squeak. Squeak. Squeak-squeak. Squeak-squeak-squeak-squeak. Moan. Squeak.

Steven opened one eye and directed it toward the nightstand. The clock read three-o-five.

Squeak . . . grunt.

How fortunate, he contemplated, that his new neighbor's bedroom was opposite his. And how wonderful that she liked to indulge in a certain libidinous activity at three in the morning. Those were definitely bedsprings bouncing rhythmically.

Pulling a pillow over his face, he decided to call a real estate agent first thing in the morning. He was going to relocate post haste.

Squeak-squeak-squeak.

He groaned.

Standing on the bed in her oversized pajamas, Meg stretched toward the ceiling with another grunt. Just a few more swipes with the rag and the paint smear would be gone. The old brass frame protested resoundingly as she shimmied the cloth briskly overhead.

What had possessed her to start painting a mural at this time of night? And on her ceiling, for crying out loud! The crick in her neck was punishment enough to remind her not to embark on such a scatterbrained project the next time her insomnia got out of hand.

She scrubbed once more and blew a red curl out of her eyes. Hopefully, Steven Kincaid, the man with the sick sense of humor, couldn't hear what she was doing. Not that she cared if it drove him crazy, but it wouldn't be very wise to get evicted before she'd had a chance to settle in.

"Bazil, the tormented cockatoo, indeed," she huffed at the small likeness of a unicorn on the ceiling. "He's a nutcase."

Mr. Rupert had confided that the businessman with the emerald eyes and unruly brown hair was a bit odd, but she'd had no idea he liked to keep company with imaginary avians. Too bad he was so attractive. She'd watched him pull into the shared driveway yesterday in his classic car, the sun glinting off the shiny hood of the hunter-green vehicle proudly. A boy's toy. That was how she viewed such an ostentatious display of wealth. He liked showing it off. The scene had reminded her of her parents, so she'd been about to turn from the kitchen window when he'd climbed out of the car.

The grace with which he'd moved was fascinating. He'd uncoiled his large body from behind the wheel and extended his arms skyward, the muscles of his upper torso straining against his white cotton shirt. His broad shoulders and chest had moved sinuously as he'd worked out the kinks, oblivious to the rapt attention of a passing woman on the sidewalk. A taut butt sat atop long legs encased in expensively cut gray pants, and her breath had actually stopped when he'd leaned down to retrieve his briefcase and jacket from the car, affording her a generous view of said behind. He'd squinted at the spring sunshine, his lashes resting darkly above hard cheekbones. A straight nose was positioned perfectly above a mouth that might have been described as stern were it not for the sensual curve of his lower lip.

Meg snapped out of her trance and scrubbed vigorously once again. She was not interested in men except in a purely aesthetic way, the artist in her unable to resist the allure of a beautifully proportioned body. If her neighbor just happened to own a body like that . . . well, it was her duty to check it out.

At twenty-six and still a virgin, Meg had vowed long ago she would not make the mistake of confusing lust with love and succumb to temptation as her parents had. That way lay misery, and she'd lived in it — been the reason for it — all her life.

Personally, she didn't understand what the whole fuss over sex was about. She'd never been enticed into a physical relationship with a man, even when a male model she'd been sketching had invited it. It was peculiar how often that had happened.

Thankfully, her days of having to fend off men who were attracted simply because she was disinterested were over.

Her spot cartoons were a success, and her income had stabilized quite nicely without her having to dip into the hated trust fund left by her grandfather.

Just as she stepped off the bed the doorbell rang. She froze, wondering who would be up at this time of night to bother someone else—except another insomniac like herself. Or a neighbor. She grimaced as a pounding started on the front door.

Meg peered through the peephole at the bare-chested, irate man in the entryway. His hair was tousled, and he'd not troubled himself to put anything on over his boxer shorts.

Leaving the chain hooked, she opened the door a crack, shielding her own loosely clad form behind it. "Yes?"

"What the hell are you doing?" he rumbled grimly. "Never mind. I know what you're doing. It's obvious."

"It is?" How could he know she'd smudged vermillion on the unicorn's tail?

"Yes, dammit. Your bedroom is right next to mine."

"Oh, I didn't realize that. I'm sorry." She closed the door and locked it as he stomped back to his own place. *Oops!*

Lifting the mass of titian curls off her heated neck, Meg scolded herself for getting so flustered at the sight of a man's semi-nude body. She'd seen more than that on absolutely gorgeous specimens, for heaven's sake. It was just a body . . . with a dusting of that same sable hair on its chest . . . and shoulders to die for.

It sure was hot for May. Fanning her face, she tiptoed off to bed.

Steven was unusually grumpy. He'd always prided himself on being a happy early riser. Now, for the first time ever, he was muttering to himself and mentally hexing the woman next door. Even after his trek out to the chilly entryway last night, the echo of what must have been some very satisfying sex had kept him awake and restless for another hour.

He was itching, that was all. Over and over, he told himself he just needed the comfort of another warm body in his bed and the physical fulfillment of a little sex. Even if it wasn't very satisfying — during or after.

Ezmerelda had sure been enjoying herself — why shouldn't he? Instead, he'd tossed and turned and cussed, slept fitfully, and awakened to stub his big toe on the dresser and nick his chin shaving. It was a hell of a night. And it was all her fault!

Wincing at the bitter taste of coffee, he thunked the mug down on the counter and snatched up his keys. He threw his suit jacket over one arm and headed for his car, certain this morning couldn't get any worse. Of course, he was wrong.

The nagging sensation of having forgotten something hit him when he slid the key into the car's ignition. His briefcase. That small item containing a mountain of information and paperwork was still propped next to the couch.

In his haste to get out of the car, he nearly tripped at the same time as he was shutting the door. A breeze gusted up simultaneously and lifted his blue silk tie into the gap, and presto, he was fastened to his car. He yanked on the handle, but the door had locked. An experimental jerk on his tie accomplished nothing.

"Ah, the joys of owning a classic car," he muttered while he gazed longingly at the keys still swinging from the ignition and his cell phone on the dash. "A bit too classic." Straining to see if anyone was within shouting distance, he twisted awkwardly from his bent position and cursed the people who designed low-slung automobiles. He closed his eyes, braced his hands on the roof, and tried to calm down, breathing deeply as he counted to ten. When he looked across the bonnet of the car again, a short, freckle-faced boy was grinning toothlessly at him. *Johnny.*

"Whatcha doin'?" quizzed the demonic youngster.

Steven, who'd had tons of experience with the sandy-haired kid, tried a disarming smile. "I was on my way to the office, but I seem to have run into a problem."

"Oh yeah?" Johnny asked. His hazel eyes darted around shiftily. The child was only nine and had developed a keen understanding of when someone was most vulnerable to a prank. He'd exhibited this trait on a regular basis, much to his parents' chagrin.

"Were you on your way to school?" Steven tried to conceal his frustration when the tiny trouble-maker peeked over the top of the car and shook his head.

"Teachers' workshop. Me and Kenny and Sly were jus' goin' to the park."

It was then that it became apparent to Steven that he was surrounded by the neighborhood scoundrels on three sides, the latter two creeping cautiously closer as they comprehended his predicament. They let their ringleader do all the talking.

Johnny rounded the car warily. "What's the matter, Mr. Kinket? Is ya stuck?"

"Mr. Kincaid," he automatically corrected. "I'm sort of stuck, yes. Would you mind knocking on that nice lady's door," he nodded to The Voice's apartment, "and asking her to come out here?"

A slow grin spread from one freckled ear to the other, and Steven cursed his rotten luck. Johnny smelled a sucker and was about to take a lick.

"How about we make a deal, Johnny? If you go up the steps to that porch and knock on the door next to mine," Steven coaxed hopefully, "I'll give you and your friends five bucks."

The kid seemed to consider that for a few seconds before he replied adultly, "Nah. Five bucks don't buy much these days—not for three of us." He glanced at his buddies and then stepped forward to poke Steven in the ribs. "Maybe if you gave us five *each* . . ." Another jab landed on his arm.

Brat! He thought and bared his teeth in a smile. "If I promise to give you five bucks each, will you go get some help?"

"You give us the money first." Johnny was nothing if not shrewd. "Then we'll knock on that lady's door for you."

Kenny and Sly edged closer and chortled along with the instigator. Both boys were slightly shorter and a bit chubby, their blond heads almost perfectly round. Steven guessed they were brothers, though he hadn't noticed them in the area before. *Johnny's new recruits.*

"I don't think I like the idea of handing over my money first. How do I know you'll keep your end of the deal?"

Johnny shrugged his thin shoulders. "We could jus' take your wallet and *all* your money. There's three of us and you're tied to your car."

Steven slapped a hand protectively over his back pocket where the leather item was clearly outlined. Kenny and Sly moved in when Johnny gave a commanding toss of the head.

Mugged by nine-year-olds. He glared at his neighbor's door one last time. *I've changed my mind – I'm never having kids.*

Mornings were Meg's favorite time of day. She loved to see the first rays of sun filtering through the curtains as she looked out the window at the waking world, a cup of herbal tea in her hand.

This morning she'd slept in later than usual due to her bout with insomnia and had risen to stumble to the shower, clumsily shedding her pajamas as she went. The warm spray had restored her senses somewhat, making the task of dressing in baggy jeans and denim shirt less complicated than she'd feared. Even knotting her shirttails together hadn't posed a major problem.

Her red ringlets still damp, she trudged barefoot to the kitchen and filled the kettle, setting it to boil while she leaned against the counter and surveyed her new home.

The old house was roomy by anyone's standards, even someone who'd spent eighteen years of her life in the lap of luxury. The kitchen was large and airy, its wooden cabinets and yellow walls cheery. Her bedroom was the ideal size for her old brass bed, two dressers, and a vanity. The bathroom had been modernized to include a shower stall as well as the claw-footed tub. A spacious living room opened off the kitchen and currently contained an ivory-colored sofa and matching chair to complement the old-fashioned shiplap paneling on the walls. The dining room was small, but she'd decided that would serve as part of her work space along with the spare bedroom.

All of her things had been stored and arranged to her satisfaction after two days of lugging and unpacking. Her friends had been more than accommodating, a fact for which she was extremely grateful.

The kettle whistled, snapping her out of her reverie. She sighed at the first sip of hot tea and wandered to the window. The sight that greeted her there was more than a little strange. Steven Kincaid was half stooped over the bonnet of his car, one hand on his behind and the other waving at three boys who were apparently blowing raspberries and dodging capture excitedly. Meg frowned when she realized the man was unable to move from his uncomfortable semi-crouch and was becoming more annoyed and harried by the second. She left her tea on the counter and went to investigate.

"Excuse me," Meg called from the top of the steps, shielding her eyes from the bright sun. "Is something wrong, Mr. Kincaid?"

The three boys scampered away at the sound of her voice, chuckling gleefully all the way down the street.

One thick, dark brow arched as the tall man scowled over his shoulder at her. "I'm attached to my car." His face and ears turned red with humiliation.

Meg, still in her bare feet, left the porch to stand beside him. He turned his gaze straight ahead, and a pang of sympathy twanged inside her when she noticed that he was, indeed, tied to his car. "How did you manage that?"

"Does it matter?" he mildly enquired, a vein in his neck prominently indicating his stress. "My tie got stuck, and the door locked on its own."

"Mmm. I can see." She peered more closely at his flushed face. He really was a handsome man, and very embarrassed. "What do you want me to do? Get your spare keys?"

"They're in my briefcase. In my apartment."

"Ah. Do you have a cell phone—or is that in your briefcase, too?"

"No, my cell phone is in my car." Then he added, "The tie was a gift from my niece—otherwise I'd just get you to cut it."

Meg looked through the windshield and sighed. "Can I call someone from my place?"

"Oh, would you?" was the sarcastic response.

"Maybe."

Heaving those wide shoulders, he bowed his head and mumbled, "Please. I can't stoop any lower to loosen and unknot the damn thing. My face hits the bonnet."

"What's the number?" she relented. The poor man had suffered enough at the hands of those rude kids. There was no reason for her to act like a juvenile.

14

The car's hostage rattled off a number and told her who to ask for. "Tell him I need him to jimmy open my door. ASAP!"

Meg jogged back inside and placed the call. On the second ring, a pleasant female voice said, "Hello."

"Hi, could I speak with JJ? It's rather urgent."

"One minute, I'll catch him before he gets in his car." The phone was dropped abruptly, and a few moments passed. Meg waited for the woman to come back. "Sorry about that. Here he is now." A low conversation took place while the receiver was transferred from one hand to another.

"Vanzant," a deep baritone rumbled tersely.

"Hello. I'm calling for Steven Kincaid." Meg quickly explained what had happened and conveyed the request for her neighbor's expeditious release.

"Stevie got his tie jammed in the door?" Laughter roared across the line as the man grasped the ridiculous situation. "I'll be right there."

Biting her quivering lip, she informed the bent prisoner that help was on the way. She couldn't resist an interested peek at his tight bottom when he leaned against the car. Poor, poor, sexy man. He was really embarrassed.

"I have another problem and I don't think it'll wait for JJ to get here." A pregnant pause followed his announcement. "I have to use the bathroom."

"Oh. Oh my." Grabbing her sides to stop the giggles from erupting, she ignored his strident objections and bolted for her apartment. Once hidden from view, she doubled over and laughed until tears streamed down her face. She had to do something. The man had to go, and she couldn't let him languish in the driveway while she stayed inside.

He didn't protest when he saw her coming with the scissors. In fact, the look of pure relief on his face said that he welcomed any solution wholeheartedly, even one that destroyed his coveted gift.

Meg carefully reached around him and cut the silky material in two, bracing his cramped frame as he straightened despite the heat that raced through her at the feel of his hard body. How strange that other men seemed to hold their warmth much easier than he did. Steven Kincaid radiated like a furnace.

"Thank you," he threw over one shoulder and ran for the front door, in a hurry to relieve himself. He stopped suddenly at the foot of the steps.

"Just go in and use my bathroom," Meg offered, seeing the fix he was in. He had no keys to open his apartment with, after all. She trailed behind him slowly, trying desperately to restrain her mirth.

Steven washed his hands and stared glumly at the rumpled, flustered image that was his reflection. He'd never been so utterly humiliated in front of a beautiful woman—a stunning, flame-haired, long-legged paragon of sensuality with the bluest eyes he'd ever seen. When he'd raised his head to find her walking toward him in that languid way she had of moving, he decided he didn't give a damn if she was a hippie or a nun. She'd knocked the wind out of him.

The Voice had ceased to exist. Now, he thought of her as simply . . . The Vision.

Rapidly drying his hands, he grinned ruefully at the triangle of blue fabric that hung pathetically below his tie knot. She was inventive. Cute. *Taken.*

There were no signs of her male companion in the bathroom. Only feminine soaps and makeup, moisturizers, and shampoo littered the counter next to the sink. That meant nothing except that her lover didn't live with her—yet.

Maybe the guy was still lounging in bed. He'd been in too

much of a hurry to relieve himself to notice if the bedroom door was shut.

Steven let loose a four-letter word and warily exited the bathroom, checking left and right before treading down the hall to the kitchen. There, calmly sipping from a mug, was The Vision. Her enormous blue eyes danced merrily as she sized him up.

"Feeling better?" she queried.

"Much." He cleared his throat. "I hope I didn't take you away from, ah, anything."

Frowning slightly, she said, "No. There's coffee if you'd like to wait for your friend here. I'm afraid all I have is instant."

He glanced furtively around but saw no evidence of her fellow *squeaker*. "No, thanks. JJ shouldn't be much longer. I'll just go back out to the car."

"Okay." The Vision narrowed her splendid eyes, thick lashes obscuring her expression. "By the way, what were those kids doing earlier?"

"Polishing their criminal techniques. Johnny and the gang are sort of a suburban mini-mob," he explained and headed for the door. "Bye."

"See ya."

Outside, Steven chastised himself for not thanking her properly. He'd make it up to her somehow. Right now, he had a big, blond PI to deal with who happened to be grinning broadly as he trained a cell phone on what was left of his buddy's tie.

"This is one for the books, Stevie." JJ snapped a picture and turned to the car. He clicked another shot of the material fluttering from the door. "I'll make duplicates for everyone we know."

"Shut up, Vanzant."

The blond PI couldn't stop one last wicked chuckle before

unlocking the car.

CHAPTER TWO

"Good day." Jonas Mackenzie tilted his chair back and laced his fingers together over a massive chest. The redhead had the nerve to grin happily as Steven plopped down in the seat opposite his desk. "Have we recovered from our little mishap this morning?"

It was nearly lunchtime and Steven had managed to avoid this conversation by sidestepping his partner's office as much as possible. The inevitable meeting could not be put off any longer.

"I have no idea what you mean."

Jonas snickered mischievously. "Vanzant called."

"Naturally." Steven unrolled his shirt sleeve and studiously began rolling it back up. "It could happen to anyone. But go ahead, have your laugh."

"I'm getting blow-ups of those pictures. Viv will love it when I tell her you strapped yourself to your beloved sportscar."

At the mention of his cousin, Steven attempted to change the subject. "How is my favorite almost-sister?"

"Dandy. How's your tie?" The sly question came out on a gasp as he gave in to more laughter.

"Once JJ freed it, I did my duty and eulogized it before burying it in the trash." Steven shook his head sadly. "It was my best tie. I ought to demand that woman next door buy me a new one."

Jonas eyed him enquiringly.

"She kept me up half the night," he explained. The image

of her making love to some faceless stud was more than a bit disturbing now that he'd met her. He brushed the thought aside. She was seeing someone, and what they did together was none of his business. Unless it woke him up at three in the morning.

"What does that have to do with you getting nabbed by your car door?"

"I wasn't alert. If I'd been sensible enough to know what I was doing, it never would have happened." The notion of the flame-haired beauty having to make up for her thoughtlessness was infinitely alluring. She could feel so bad about it that she offered to give him full body massages. He was going to have to work on her compassionate side, he decided. It would have done wonders for Baz.

"What are you thinking about, Kincaid? You're grinning like the cat who got the cream." Jonas narrowed his gaze. "How attractive is she?"

"Who?"

"Your neighbor."

Steven shivered dramatically. "Ugh! The woman is the scariest creature I've ever crossed paths with." His frown was convincing. "Warts and everything."

"Yeah?"

"Ooooooh, yeah. Not very appetizing at all." Steven had had years to perfect his deadpan expression. It came in handy when lying through his teeth.

"That's too bad. It's time you settled down." Jonas lowered his eyebrows comically. "There must be one unattached woman hanging around who's willing to take you."

"Jeez, you sound like your wife—and the rest of our family. Did it ever occur to you that the problem is not with me? That there might be a slim chance that the women of this province don't know a good thing when they see it?"

It took a full minute for the other man to control his guffaws. Wiping tears from his eyes, he declared, "Maybe you should expand your search to include the entire Atlantic region."

"Maybe I will."

"Or at the very least, look next door," Jonas added astutely.

Steven shuddered for effect. "Absolutely not!"

The day seemed to drag after that. Once back in his own office, Steven ignored his common sense and called a florist. He hoped his neighbor liked roses. Lots of them.

The doorbell rang just as Meg was completing a sketch of a man bent over his car. He was gripping his snared tie, beads of sweat popping out on his forehead while he braced one foot against the door in an exhaustive attempt to escape. The caption read — *The thing most feared by the male species — man-eating vehicles.*

She grinned to herself, moved around the raised drawing table and out to the kitchen. Peeping through the window above the sink, she was surprised to see a van sporting a popular logo in the driveway.

The delivery man smiled affably when she took the enormous bouquet of red roses and tipped him. She found a vase that had been shoved in one of the cupboards and set it on the counter, placing the long-stemmed flowers carefully so as not to crush any of the exquisite petals. Burying her nose in the fragrant blooms, she inhaled and closed her eyes.

Roses. No one had ever given her flowers of any kind but once. That had been the time her father had begged off from attending her high school graduation and sent her a bunch of orchids. His new wife — number four, if Meg remembered correctly — had persuaded him to fly to Aruba for a month. Harry Layton's whims and those of his wives had always come before the needs of his only child. She'd grown used to it . . . and tired of it.

Pushing away the memory that never failed to sadden her, she searched for a card. Slipping it from the tiny envelope, she scanned it quickly and laughed.

I hope you can forgive my rudeness this morning. I didn't thank you enough for rescuing me – S.K.

Meg strolled back to her drawing table. Using an eraser, she altered the uncanny likeness of the man next door. A few minutes later, her subject was bespectacled and bald. She couldn't share the poor man's embarrassment with the whole world after he'd sent her roses now, could she?

By late afternoon, the mural on her bedroom ceiling was near completion. Unicorns danced across a darkened sky that glittered with silver stars. A small garden sat in the middle, an explosion of earthly colors creating a welcome sanctuary in the midst of the galaxy's uncertain weightlessness. It was an ethereal utopia.

Meg sighed. She was good at producing fantasies, had become adept at dreaming up her own. Unfortunately, hers had often included two loving parents who acknowledged her existence simply because she was theirs and not trotted out occasionally to be viewed by acquaintances who cast an obligatory glance her way and said something like, "My, Alice, your daughter is turning out quite nicely – under the circumstances."

Those *circumstances* had hounded Meg all her life. Her parents had been forced to marry after a spontaneous tryst for which neither of them had been prepared. So *overcome with passion* were they that birth control had been the last thing on their minds.

Years of fights and separations had ensued, always with Meg caught in the middle. Finally, when she was ten, Alice and Harry decided to go their separate ways. Of course, there was no argument over which of them should take responsibility for the child. Both parents had just assumed the other would seize custody and control of the whopping trust fund that came with it. Well, neither was poor enough to make such a sacrifice in Meg's eyes. Harry had grudgingly allowed her to live with him while he went through a parade of Mrs. Laytons, and Alice had flounced off to Paris to live with her newest lover.

Meg hadn't seen either of them for nearly six years—her choice. She'd had all the blame and emotional neglect she could stomach at twenty. After Harry skipped out of going to the milestone event that was her college graduation—the early one she'd made herself sick striving for just so he'd be impressed by her brilliance—she'd packed her things and taken enough money to keep her going for a few months and left.

As far as she knew, no one had tried tracking her down. She hadn't said in her brief note where she was headed or that she'd be in touch, but she hadn't attempted to cover up her location either.

The doorbell sounded, and she dragged herself from the bed and her memories, trudging wearily to let Olaf in.

Should he ring her bell and ask if she liked the flowers? Steven climbed the few steps to the shared porch. He stood and contemplated his neighbor's door. Would he seem too eager? Too needy? Probably. He continued to waver for a while longer before reaching for the button.

The *thump-thump* of his heartbeat sped up significantly when he detected movement behind the frosted glass panes. He drew a steadying breath and swept a hand through his hair, hoping he didn't look as nervous as he felt.

The door swung open to reveal a huge blond guy who

was only half dressed. Steven stared blankly at the muscle-bound Mr. Universe, and his shoulders drooped. The mystery *squeaker.*

"Hi. Is, ah . . ." He swallowed, realizing he still didn't know the woman's name.

The giant offered a beefy hand. "I am Olaf."

Steven shook the man's paw and tried to peer past him. "Nice to meet you. I live next door." He gestured helpfully, not sure how versed Olaf was in English.

"Ja, ja." Arms as thick as tree stumps crossed over *very* developed pectorals. "She is . . . how do you say . . . occupied?" Olaf smiled, baring a set of strong, feral teeth.

I'll bet she is. The notion of this big oaf in his neighbor's bed left a bitter taste in his mouth. "I won't disturb her then."

"Ja." The large head bobbed once.

Then, as Steven turned slowly toward his own door, Olaf grinned wolfishly and shut him out.

"Who was it?" Meg asked absently as the gorgeous model resumed his position on the stool. Olaf was a dear friend who was putting himself through school by trading on his Nordic appearance. He was a sweet man with a definite feel for the outrageous and often liked to pull one's leg. He was part Swede, part Norwegian, part German, and all male.

"The guy from next door," Olaf supplied in flawless English. He'd mastered three languages since coming to Canada and had picked up all sorts of mannerisms.

"Mr. Kincaid? Why didn't he come in?"

Olaf shrugged his impressive shoulders. "Beats me. He may have thought you were intimately indisposed."

Meg shot him a suspicious look. "Why would he think that?" Not that she cared.

"Well, here I am, riveting in my attractiveness," he innocently remarked, "and you are nowhere to be seen. What could the man think?"

She lifted a hand in dismissal. "It doesn't matter. We're finished here."

"Ah, Megan, why is it so hard for you to be interested in men? You are not gay, are you?" Olaf pulled on his shirt and eyed her closely.

She smiled a little. "No." Handing him the sketch to add to his portfolio, she added, "I'm just not concerned with those messy entanglements."

"You are happy being alone?"

"I have my friends, my work. Yes, I'm perfectly content."

"If you were not such a good pal, I would show you what you are missing." Olaf winked. "Perhaps Mr. Kincaid is a candidate for that job." He chuckled when she couldn't hide a blush. "He did seem a bit miffed when I opened the door. Maybe he has his eye on you."

Meg scowled. "We don't know each other."

"He sent you roses."

"You were nosy enough to read the card!"

"I care for you," he said apologetically, "as all your friends do. You are lonely, Meg, and there is always a sadness in you."

"Go home, Doctor. I have to fix supper." It was habit to deflect the genuine concern with a smile.

Olaf took the hint and departed, whistling *I'm in the Mood*.

Meg locked the front door and leaned tiredly against it. She had to give her friends points for a valiant effort. They were boggled when it came to her lack of enthusiasm over dating. Most of them were married or engaged and had set about using their matchmaking skills on her. She just hadn't been tempted.

An image of Steven Kincaid burst forth, tousled hair falling across his forehead, green eyes flashing whilst he fought a losing battle with his vehicle. Now that could be temptation . . . *if* she was a woman to be drawn to his type or any other — which she wasn't.

He was an odd man anyway. How in the world did he succeed in snaring himself like that?

She sighed and returned to her drawing table. The cartoon she'd finished earlier had stayed hidden beneath some other sketches. She pulled it out now and studied it, debating whether or not to replace the bald man with her neighbor again. Believing that to even consider it gave her dormant libido too much importance, she buried the caricature quickly and put it out of her mind.

The clock on his nightstand read twelve-o-two. So far, he hadn't heard any squeaking emanating from the bedroom abutting his.

Steven yanked irritably on the blankets.

Maybe they'd gone to Olaf's place. Not that her whereabouts were any of his business.

He thumped the pillow into shape and stuffed it under his neck. He was tired. He *was.* Sugar plum fairies were dancing in his head . . . and visions of a redheaded siren making love to a beefy blond. Tossing the bed clothes aside, he sat on the edge of the mattress and rolled his shoulders.

The adjacent apartment was still silent.

He ambled to the kitchen and searched the refrigerator for a snack. While he was in the middle of constructing a ham, cheese, lettuce, tomato, and pastrami sandwich, his ear quirked involuntarily.

A distant hum reverberated through the duplex, the source of which he could not identify. He straightened and listened for a few seconds as it grew louder and then faded abruptly.

Shaking his head in confusion, he went back to his lunch. He could have sworn he'd heard something. Not like a human noise. Something mechanical?

The counter was cool and hard when he propped himself against it. It was also vibrating ominously. He shoved the last bite of the monster sandwich in his mouth and pivoted to stare curiously at the area surrounding the sink.

The hum returned, this time rising in pitch until it reached a threatening groan. The counter shook visibly, every spoon and cup jostling nearer the edge as if disturbed by an earthquake. An earthquake? Did they have those in Newfoundland? No. But plumbing disasters were universal.

Almost as if the idea itself had given birth to the actual event, the kitchen wall shuddered around the sink and a loud pop preceded a geyser of cold water spewing wildly from the exploded tap, drenching his unclothed body with the impetus of a million tiny whips.

He hooted. He howled. He tried to stem the frigid flow with his hands. In a panic, he raced from the apartment and pounded on The Vision's door, gasping and dripping while he shivered uncontrollably in the porch. Steven banged again—hard!

"What are you doing!?" The woman obviously had been sleeping and was not amused at being disturbed. Her red curls swirled about pajama-clad shoulders, the vibrant sight making him forget why he'd rushed over. "Good Lord! What happened?" she demanded, aghast.

Steven flipped the sopping hair from his eyes and chattered frostily, "Not now. Just tell me where the damned valve is to shut off the water before the entire city drowns."

"How should I know? I just moved in, remember?" She sped past him and into his place, her blue nightshirt flapping. He followed and tried not to notice the creamy glimpse of leg afforded by the loose outfit.

The water had reached the living room, and he was thankful that God had bestowed him with the presence of mind to realize how dangerous it was to leave electrical appliances plugged in. He rapidly dealt with them all in that room before dashing into the kitchen and doing the same.

The Vision was courageously attempting to get underneath the sink with a wrench she must have appropriated from the broom closet, undaunted by the freezing temperature of the spray.

Steven splashed in beside her and shone a flashlight he'd grabbed from the top of the refrigerator onto the pipes. They bumped heads and shoulders, cursing above the wet fracas.

A second later, all was silent.

As his neighbor stood and tossed the wrench on the counter, he wondered vaguely if all oversized pajama tops looked as good on half-drowned women. The cotton material clung to her full, high breasts, outlining the pebbled nipples erotically. His groin tightened in sharp awareness, the cold fabric of his shorts no deterrent to the surprising jolt of desire.

The soggy picture before him raised her hands to comb the drizzling hair off her face. Cobalt-blue eyes blazed from beneath her finely arched brows. She sloshed through the almost ankle-deep water to the phone mounted on the wall.

"What's the landlord's number?"

Steven's useless mouth shivered, "Uh, I dunno. I haven't used it much."

Carefully, The Vision replaced the receiver. "I'll go back to my place and call him." She sneezed. "You'd better dry off before you catch a—choo!—cold." Then, walking stiffly, she left him kicking himself for behaving like a helpless idiot.

The man was a walking disaster. Meg lifted her face to the hot shower. It warmed her icy bones as she mentally listed, for the umpteenth time, all the reasons why she stayed away from men.

Not that he hadn't been exceedingly adorable in his sodden underwear, but Steven Kincaid was definitely off limits. Any man who could look captivating and sexy yet completely incompetent at the same time was a certain lust-trap. Even the chills invading her body hadn't discouraged the flash of hunger storming through her as he'd dripped magnificently all over his kitchen tiles.

She twisted the faucet as if switching off a television, exiling the images of the last hour to the back of her mind.

After drying her hair, she sipped hot chocolate on her couch and glumly resigned herself to another sleepless night. She'd actually been dozing when The Hapless Wonder had begun pounding on her door.

Poor guy, she mused, he really did have a rotten day.

A giggle escaped Meg's lips, a sure sign that she was overly tired.

The doorbell rang, and she tensed, stupefied that he might be caught up in another little drama. Surely he would have gone to bed by now. Hadn't she heard the grouchy plumber come and go?

"I saw your light on," Steven sheepishly explained when she opened the door. "I figured I might as well apologize now. I should have just called the landlord and let the place flood while I waited." He'd changed into gray sweats and tennis shoes, his hair now only slightly damp from the ordeal.

Meg smiled a little at his discomfort and took pity on him. "Forget it. I'm a lousy sleeper anyway. I was just having some hot chocolate before trying it again. Want some?" She left the door wide and padded to the kitchen, leaving him the option to follow or not. It didn't matter to her if he came inside, she firmly told her fluttering pulse.

"You'll have to forgive me," he said as she handed him a steaming mug, "but I still don't know your name."

"Meg. Megan Layton." She smiled and led him into the living room. "Did the plumber say what the problem was?"

Steven glanced around with interest before folding his large body into a chair. "Old pipes. He said Rupert will need to get them replaced or keep having trouble."

"Oh." She frowned. "Shouldn't I be having the same problems if my place is adjoining yours?"

"Not since the last tenant had the foresight to demand our plumbing be separated. I didn't mind my shower going cold on me occasionally, but he couldn't take to it. When the work was done it involved replacing most of his pipes." He eyed her somewhat guiltily. "Your nose is a bit red. If you catch pneumonia, I'm going to be your nurse twenty-four hours a day."

Meg laughed. "Don't worry, I'm hardly ever sick. Not since grade school, in fact."

"Where did you learn to be so handy with a wrench?" His voice was nice, deep with a raspy quality that she liked.

"Necessity. I've been on my own for a few years. Olaf — you met him earlier — also taught me how to use a set of screwdrivers, a hammer, a pair of pliers, and a baseball bat. He's very protective."

"Your boyfriend?" Steven's gaze became decidedly more alert when he posed the question.

Chuckling wryly, she shook her head. "No, a very good friend. I sketch him now and then to update his portfolio, and he teaches me German."

"Ah, that's what you were doing this evening. I thought . . ." He flushed endearingly and let the sentence fade.

"Mmm." She sipped the last drop from her mug. "That's what he wanted you to think."

"You said you sketch?"

"Not models so much anymore. I do spot cartoons—like you see in magazines—and some painting. Which is what I was attempting to do last night when I woke you." She grimaced. "Sorry about that."

"Painting?"

"Well, I smeared and was rubbing it off. That's why I was making the bed shake. I put a mural on my ceiling."

Steven's eyes darkened to a deeper emerald shade, the laughter lines at the corners crinkling attractively. She thought he must smile a lot.

"So you don't have a boyfriend?" he asked, directing his attention to the liquid in his cup. His casual demeanor didn't alert her to the possibility that he might be interested.

"No boyfriend."

"Fiancé?"

"No."

"Husband?"

Pause. "You're awfully inquisitive."

He shrugged.

"No," she sighed, "no husband. I'm not the marrying kind."

That response earned her a quirk of the eyebrow and a crooked grin. "I thought all women were."

"Not this one." Meg studied him soberly. "Some of us just don't have good examples to follow."

"That's a shame."

This time it was her turn to shrug, feigning indifference.

Steven's voice dropped to an intimate murmur when he suggested, "If you're free some night soon, maybe we could catch a movie or have supper. At a restaurant, that is. I'm as much a danger in the kitchen as anywhere else."

"I noticed."

His shoulders shook with laughter, the sound warming Meg from the inside out. This man could be the one to bring about her downfall, her headlong plunge into the forbidden land of *overwhelming physical desire* as she'd heard Alice say to a friend above her young daughter's head. Well, her grown daughter was not going there.

As if sensing her sudden withdrawal, he got to his feet and thanked her for the hot chocolate. "The offer for supper is still open if you're up for it."

"I'm really busy these days. Perhaps when I'm not so tied up." Softening the dismissal with a polite smile, she held open the door. She could see that he didn't believe her excuse but was willing to let her off with it.

"When you're settled in then. Thanks for the help with the water and everything." He hesitated momentarily before dropping a swift kiss on her mouth. "Goodnight, Meg."

Meg, whose eyes were as round as saucers, muttered something that must have made sense and gaped at his retreating back.

Of all the nerve! How arrogant, how presumptuous that he would dare make a pass . . . She touched her still tingling mouth. Then, as she chastised her rampant hormones for making her think she'd actually liked his kiss, she slammed the door forcefully and stalked off to bed.

Steven smiled at his attractive single neighbor as she came up the steps toward him. "Need help?"

"No," she denied, as expected. Staggering beneath the weight of her groceries and tote bag, she tottered up the stairs and clumsily tried to unlock her door without setting a thing down. Finally, she relinquished the key to him and stumbled inside with her load, apparently none too pleased with having to accept his assistance.

He shouldn't have kissed her—not even that little peck that paled in comparison to what he'd really wanted to do last night. He'd been giddy with relief when he'd discovered her relationship with Olaf was purely platonic, unable to contain his pleasure when she'd said there was no man in her life. Unfortunately, he feared that his enthusiasm had put her off—as exhibited by the slamming of her door after he'd left and her dispirited greeting now. At thirty-seven, he was old enough to know he shouldn't be so pushy. But her mouth had tasted even sweeter than he could have imagined. If he apologized for being so forward it would be with absolutely no sincerity. So he didn't bother.

"Water all cleaned up?" Meg asked when he trailed in behind her.

"Mostly. The carpet's still damp in the living room and hallway."

She stored her purchases in record time and set the kettle to boil. "Tea?"

"No, thanks." He watched her move around the kitchen, intrigued by the snug fit of her jeans. His throat clogged, so he cleared it loudly. "Rupert was by."

"Hmm?" Perched on a chair, she darted a glance his way and motioned for him to join her.

"My apartment is about to be invaded. The plumber has advised him that the place will be unlivable while he replaces the pipes. I'll have to stay somewhere else."

"Oh?" The woman had the audacity to look relieved at the news.

Steven scowled. "I'm being ousted, uprooted."

"For how long?" she queried, seemingly unable to suppress her excitement.

"A year."

Meg blinked. "That long?"

"A month—maybe."

Disappointed, her mouth formed another "Oh".

Growling, he stated, "I'm not that bad."

"You're a little accident prone."

"Not normally. It's been that kind of week."

Placing her elbows on the table, she cupped her face and observed him as if he were an organism under a microscope.

He squirmed.

"You shouldn't have done it." The comment was softly spoken but adamant.

"What?" Steven turned on his blank look, but he knew she was referring to the kiss.

"Ambushed me."

"I didn't ambush you. You stood right there," he jabbed a thumb over his shoulder, "and made yourself impossible to resist."

"How did I do that?" Meg appeared genuinely perplexed.

"You . . . stood . . . right . . . there."

"I often stand there. It's my doorway."

The kettle shrieked, and she went to shut it off. Steven came up behind her and lifted her hair, leaning close to whisper against her neck, "I didn't want to kiss you that way. I wanted to do it like this." His mouth found her cheek. "And this." Her jaw. "And this." His teeth nipped her earlobe gently before he pulled it into his mouth.

"I'm not interested." Her protest was faint.

"Not even a little, Meggie?" Steven slid his hands around until they rested just below her breasts, observing through half-closed eyes their rapid rise and fall beneath her thin cotton shirt. He pressed the hard ridge of his arousal to her bottom and rocked back and forth slowly, letting her feel how badly he wanted her. Meg's head fell back limply onto his shoulder, and she moaned, the wisp of sound urging him to lower his mouth to the side of her slender neck once more. He gasped harshly when she arched into him and turned her body so that he had access to her parted lips.

As he lifted her onto the counter, he fused his mouth to hers. Distantly, he thought that he'd never tasted any woman as glorious as she. Her tongue slipped along his, the velvety heat searing a path to his soul. She had an essence that was uniquely hers, a touch of honey and spice that he savored greedily, lost in the intensity of their embrace.

"I meant it when I said I wasn't interested," she panted against his mouth.

"I believe you."

"Oh good. I mean, we don't even know each other." Her glazed eyes stared into his for a second longer. Then she grabbed him by the hair and kissed him again. "I wouldn't want you to misunderstand."

"Mmm-hmm."

"This is just a kiss, right?"

"Uh-huh." He ground his hips into her mindlessly. "Just a kiss."

Meg pushed hard at his chest. "Stop that!"

"This?"

"Yesssss—that."

Steven stopped. "Unwrap your legs from my waist, Meggie. That's much too distracting." One more sweep of his lips across hers and he'd release her, he vowed. In the middle of breaking his promise, he realized vaguely that someone was knocking on the door. Or rather, someone was knocking on the door*frame* . . . inside the apartment.

"Am I interrupting?" came the heavily accented question. "The door was open, so I came on in. That is okay, *ja*?"

"Hello, Olaf." Meg managed to speak while blushing profusely. "You've met Mr. Kincaid, haven't you?"

"Hi, Olaf," Steven threw in the general vicinity of the door, not taking his eyes from hers. "Meg and I were about to have some . . . tea."

"*Ja*, I can smell something brewing. What is that flavor?"

"Passion fruit."

Olaf roared hilariously.

"Meg was just showing me how overjoyed she is that I'll be bunking with her for a month."

The look on her face was priceless, a study in amazement. "What?"

"Rupert said you have a spare room."

"I don't even know you!"

Steven eyed her legs pointedly. They were still around his hips.

"Before this, I mean."

"Last night doesn't count?" He pretended to be hurt.

Olaf chortled from his new position at the table. "Meg, you took advantage of the man and are now refusing him a place to stay?" He *tsked* sorrowfully. "I had thought you a better woman than that."

"He can't stay here. You can't," she insisted, turning her attention back to Steven. "Don't you have a relative or a friend who could put you up?"

"Certainly. But none who would put up *with* me."

"I'm not obliged to share my space with you, mister."

"Not even to make up for getting me stuck in my car door?"

Her vivid blue eyes were enormous. "That was my fault?"

Nodding, he stepped back, grateful his body had returned to its normal size. Olaf was evidently waiting for his explanation with a sympathetic ear. "She was painting in the middle of the night. It kept me up and ruined my morning concentration. Fatigued, I lurched beside my car and locked my best tie in the door. You know how it is."

"I do, I do." Olaf grinned at him, discerning his intended goal. "I was telling her just yesterday that she needed company."

Meg leaped from the counter, stomped down the hall, and bolted herself in her room.

Steven shot a puzzled look at his newfound ally. "Is she going to be a tough nut to crack?"

Olaf sighed. "Be patient—and careful of her. I'm not the only one who'll be watching."

"Understood. I don't need to leave my apartment for another five days. Help me work on her," he implored. "You know her best."

Shaking his head mournfully, the big man replied, "That would be underhanded. You don't need help. The roses were a nice touch. She put them next to her bed."

CHAPTER THREE

"How utterly ridiculous!" Meg stormed at Olaf once she'd heard Mr. It's Your Fault I Got Stuck In My Door leave through hers. "You can't possibly agree that I should let that man stay with me. He could be a criminal for all we know." She paced back and forth in agitation, the very idea of spending a month in the same place as Steven seeming preposterous and totally inappropriate.

"He isn't a criminal. While you were hiding, I called the numbers of both his business partner and his mother. They had nothing but good things to say about him. Janey is very excited about you."

"Janey?"

"Mrs. Kincaid and her husband are planning a visit just to meet you." Olaf smiled pleasantly. "That was a long-distance call, by the way."

"And where will they stay if his place is uninhabitable?" Meg felt as if the walls were closing in. Did the man next door plan on *chasing* her?

"He has twin sisters who live across town and a cousin who is married to his partner."

"Then why doesn't he stay with *them*?"

"Well," Olaf drawled thoughtfully, "as I understand it, the cousin is pregnant and doesn't need the stress, the sisters are living together and busy with their careers, the hotels are a waste of money, and he wants to get to know you."

Meg stooped over to glare at her friend. "Don't you think he's a little pushy? And weird?"

"Determined and unusual. It would take someone like that to shake you up."

"I'm not shook up."

"You were—what's the phrase—all over him like a cheap suit when I walked in."

Sputtering, she exclaimed, "You think I'm cheap? And he started that."

Olaf got to his feet and gripped her upper arms consolingly. "You are going down, Megan. Face it. As a friend I can only stand by and hope that the fall is relatively painless." He gave her forehead a brotherly peck. "I left the book you wanted on the table. Goodbye."

"You're deserting me? Leaving me at the mercy of that *klutz*?"

"Be gentle with him."

Meg locked the door after he'd gone and tried to calm her frayed nerves. There was no way she could tolerate having Steven underfoot. He'd be a pest, a nuisance. A potently attractive nuisance who could kiss like the dickens—not that she had much to compare it with. His mouth had been firm and sensual, teasing past the barriers she'd erected between herself and the opposite sex years ago. He'd smelled marvelous, too, his cologne subtle yet exciting. And his hands . . . oh God, those hard, capable hands . . .

No. He couldn't stay with her, not if she wanted to keep the promise she'd made to herself as a child. No man was ever going to make her lose her cool like she'd let him do today. Not ever. She always had control of her body's reactions and her emotions. The incident this afternoon was an aberration.

Having mostly convinced herself that it could have been any man who'd set off the curious response in her—and she was certain it was only curiosity—she forced her mind to return to the countless wedding ceremonies she'd attended.

Her father's, her mother's, her father's, et cetera. Of course, there were also the spur-of-the-moment weddings that she'd missed — thankfully.

Then again, who said Steven was interested in marriage? Maybe he just wanted a fling. How convenient for him that his target was right on his front step. Whatever he intended, he was out of luck. Neither scenario appealed to Meg. Not at all.

But he sure can kiss . . .

She sighed heavily.

Steven had written down her number before leaving her place and was now counting the rings as he waited for her to pick up. He had the feeling she might try to ignore him. He let the phone ring . . . and ring . . . and ring.

"Yes?" Meg snapped in his ear.

"Ouch! Do you have one of those tempers that redheads are notorious for? 'Cause my partner is a redhead, and he's not nearly as uptight as you are."

"I do have a temper. It's vile."

"Hmm. We'll have to work on that before I move in."

"You can't stay here. I don't know you. Go stay with your sisters."

This was going to be a long argument, he knew. Settling more comfortably on the couch, he informed her, "Caro is designing a kitchen in one of their rentals while Cass is dry-walling a bathroom in the same unit. They need to concentrate. They can't take me unless I sleep on the couch anyway."

"Or won't."

"Whatever."

"Look, Mr. —"

"Steven."

"*Steven*, you can't just shove your way into a woman's

home. It's harassment." She sounded inflexible.

"You have a few days to get used to me."

"I ... don't ... want ... to ... get ... used ... to ... you. I ... don't ... want ... anything ... to ... do ... with ... you."

He coaxed, "You want to do lots with me. You're a fabulous kisser, incidentally, and when you moaned that way—"

"A gentleman wouldn't remind me." Meg's voice held a quiver, as if she was having trouble breathing.

"I don't claim to be one where you're concerned, but I'll try from now on."

"That's good of you. If you make another pass, I'll smack you."

Steven laughed wickedly. "If you're into that sort of thing ..."

She hung up.

He dialed again. "I'm sorry. That was rude," he said when she finally answered. "Can I take you out?"

"No, I have work to do."

"I'll bring supper over."

Meg hesitated. "Not tonight."

"Tomorrow." He pictured her chewing her bottom lip as he'd noticed her doing right before he'd kissed her that afternoon. "We can go out somewhere."

"Nothing fancy."

"Suits me. I'm a hamburger guy myself." Relief at her small concession swept over him. "About six?" If he could wait that long until he saw her again.

"Fine. Goodbye."

The dial tone buzzed before he got a farewell out of his smiling mouth.

Miss Layton was not indifferent. Not by a long shot. He'd have to tread very cautiously and be patient, as Olaf had so obligingly counseled. He got the impression Meg was soured on marriage, an issue which he resolved to explore in the future. But for now, a simple calorie-laden meal and some light conversation was probably all she would allow. He'd talk her around to her feelings about matrimony after that.

"So, are you originally from St. John's?" Steven bit into his second cheeseburger and tried not to stare at the tantalizing expanse of skin above her neckline. The swell of her breasts peeked over the navy dress, scooped enticingly to drive a man crazy with longing. The thin straps yielded a view of smooth shoulders, and he was grateful to whatever genius had come up with the notion of short hemlines. Her legs went on forever, and her slender feet were encased in low-heeled pumps.

"Originally." She tucked a wayward curl behind an ear and glanced around the park. The place was filled with children and parents playing in the warm evening sun. Newfoundlanders were enjoying a bit of an early summer and crossing fingers that the rarity would last. "I moved over to Nova Scotia with my father when I was ten. I only moved back a few years ago."

"How old did you say you were?" Getting her to impart personal information was like pulling teeth. At last, he was making some progress.

"I didn't. I'm twenty-six," she relented then, almost grinning. "And you?"

"Thirty-seven." A slight age gap, he conceded, but not an enormous one.

"Is it just you and your sisters?" Her sweet mouth captured the straw in her soda, the sucking motion mesmerizing him. "Steven?"

"Oh, sorry. I have four younger brothers—all of them

married with kids."

"Must be nice," Meg wistfully remarked, "to have a bunch of siblings."

"I take it you're an only child?"

"Mmm-hmm." She shot him a look before changing the subject. "You own an electronics firm, don't you?"

"Half-ownership. Jonas, my partner, recently tied the knot with my cousin." He told her a little about his family and growing up in Bay de Chance, his university years, and how he, JJ, and Jonas had maintained their close friendship ever since. Then, in an effort to learn more about her, he back-tracked and probed, "Are your parents still living?"

Meg nodded once but said no more. Her eyes were shuttered, not permitting him to gauge her expression. "Do you want those fries?"

"Nope. I'm stuffed."

"I should say so. Two burgers, onion rings, and a donut. Where do you put it?"

"This is just a snack. I'm trying to be polite. Besides, I want to stop at that ice cream shop we passed on the way here." He grinned as she rolled her lovely eyes skyward.

"Mmm." She exhaled and patted her stomach. "That was good. Thanks for taking me out."

Steven narrowly avoided choking on his cola. "I had to practically drag you."

"Well, it's not as if this is a date or anything."

"The hell it isn't," he grumbled.

"It *isn't*."

"We'll see."

"How?"

"If I kiss you goodnight it's a bona fide date."

Meg peeped at him from beneath dark lashes. "If I call it a date — you don't kiss me," she stipulated cagily.

"Uh-uh. The labeling of this event isn't worth the sacrifice. I want a smooch."

"Drop it."

"All right." But he meant to feel those delectable lips against his before the night was over. He'd been fantasizing about nothing else for the last twenty-four hours. "So, how often do you see your folks?"

Daintily sipping the remains of her drink, she arched an elegant eyebrow. "You keep poking around there."

"You keep avoiding the topic."

"Which, of course, causes you to pry even more," she supplied caustically.

Steven made a face. "What can I say? One of my best friends is a PI. It rubs off."

"Don't quit your day job."

"How often do you see them?"

"I don't," Meg said. "Satisfied?"

Confused, he prompted, "Why not? Can't they afford the trip?"

"They can, a zillion times over probably. We just don't have much in common."

Something flashed in her eyes that told him it went far deeper than that, but he decided not to push it this time around. He simply couldn't imagine not having anything to talk about with his own parents.

"There's a story here," he muttered comically.

"Well, it's old and very boring." Meg gathered up their trash and deposited it in a nearby bin. "Thanks for supper." Apparently, his interrogation had rattled her, making her movements uncharacteristically stilted.

"You're welcome. How about dessert?"

They strolled to the nearby ice cream vendor and bought two strawberry cones.

The walk back to his car was made in companionable silence, each of them enjoying the waning sunlight as they ambled along.

A little boy of about four was running gleefully toward them and tripped suddenly, falling flat on his stomach. Meg rushed over to him and stood him upright, cooing tenderly as she brushed the dirt from his tiny knees. The mother came over to claim her son and smiled at Meg, chatting a minute before going off again.

"Cute, isn't he?" she whimsically observed.

"You like kids." That was a plus. He definitely wanted a batch of the monsters now that he'd recovered from the Johnny scare.

"I sit for a couple of friends. I'm an honorary aunt. I don't plan on having any of my own."

Uh-oh . . . we'll need to do something about that.

"This is a beautiful car." Meg ran a hand lightly over the leather upholstery. She'd thought it was a showpiece, a status symbol, but he plainly loved the machine and took great care of it.

"My cousin restored it. It was her first." The pride in his voice was unmistakable, more for the cousin than the car. "Her father was a mechanic, and she turned out to be a grease monkey in her spare time."

"You're close?"

He dipped his head and steered effortlessly through traffic as he said, "Viv was orphaned when she was ten. A drunk driver ran into her parents' car. She came to live with us and for some reason gravitated toward me and the twins more than the rest of the family. Now, she's happily married and expecting."

Meg stared at him a moment longer, envisioning how he must have taken his little cousin under his wing. The fondness with which he described her created a twinge of something she identified as envy. Certainly it wasn't jealousy. The man was free to dote on whomever he liked. Viv was only his cousin, after all. Not that she gave a fig where his attentions lay.

Scolding herself for her contrariness, she kept quiet for the remainder of the drive, muttering responses when necessary. Finally, he turned onto their street and parked in the driveway.

Dusk was falling around them, and the only sounds were the muted cries of children romping in the gardens nearby. Meg reached for the door handle and threw a hasty "See ya later!" over her shoulder before scrambling from the car. She wasn't fast enough to beat him inside, however, and was a tad piqued when his warm hand clasped her wrist as she fumbled with the lock.

"We didn't settle the small matter of a kiss." Steven's eyes darkened as his gaze dropped to her mouth.

"Yes, we did."

"No."

"All right," she capitulated. "Here." Thrusting her cheek forward, she waited for a civilized peck.

Steven laughed dryly. "Not a chance, Meggie." He lowered his head and brushed his lips over hers. He touched her nowhere else, concentrating intimately on only her mouth. Gradually, she forgot that she was supposed to pull away at the first available opportunity and let herself slip instead, into the cloak of rapture he was weaving. Her mouth trembled, and she kissed him back, seeking to stoke the fire that no man had ever ignited but him. She welcomed the invasion of his tongue eagerly, a helpless moan leaving her throat when he stroked her over and over.

Cool air drifted across her flushed skin, rousing her from the pleasurable sensations raging through her body. An inch now separated Steven's mouth and hers. His expression was unreadable, and he stared through heavy-lidded eyes at the wanton woman she knew she must resemble.

"Hey, Mr. Kinket!" intruded a strident voice. "My dad says you shouldn't do that in public."

Meg focused her gaze sharply on the freckled boy at the bottom of the steps. "Your father is right. Perhaps he should have a chat with Mr. Kincaid."

The kid she recognized as Johnny snickered. "Yeah, I think he should."

"Johnny, don't you have any butterflies to de-wing?" Steven asked in a conversational tone.

Happy to have his attention diverted, Meg squeezed into her apartment and shut him out.

What had she been thinking? She flopped against the door. Behaving in such a foolish way with *him* was idiotic. He was too handsome, too funny, too damned attractive for *her* own good. The best thing to do from now on was to avoid him at all costs, never go within ten feet of him—not even sniff his cologne.

Closing her eyes, she ran her tongue along her bottom lip, still tasting him there. She groaned. This had to stop.

Half an hour later, she was curled up on her bed with the thriller she'd borrowed from Olaf, trying desperately to make sense of the jumbled words when the phone rang. She ignored it and let the voice mail cut in, having turned on the blasted thing in a fit of irritation. Technology had its advantages—like dodging the neighbor.

The roses he'd sent were sitting on her night table in full bloom, their prominent position in her bedroom mocking her coolness. She'd put them where she could smell them first thing in the morning and last thing at night. Well, it *was* the only bunch of roses she'd ever been given, she justified grouchily. It wasn't as if they really meant anything. Except that he was a very thoughtful man . . . and she loved roses.

She got up and padded to the phone, hitting a button to

retrieve her message.

"I wish you hadn't slammed the door like that, Meggie. Johnny is now telling the neighborhood what a dork I am." Steven sighed into the phone. "Please call me when you listen to this."

"Next message," said the speaker phone.

"Preferably soon."

"Next message."

"Before I'm too old to lift the receiver."

Meg couldn't contain a smile — but she wouldn't call back.

"The Gilberg deal is a rave, buddy. We finally managed to iron out all the kinks, and the feedback is positive." Jonas slapped him on the back as they stepped onto the elevator. Jabbing the button for their floor, he continued, "The software is going to be a hit with the learning disabled and — hopefully, we can start planning that trip to Saturn any day now."

"Mmm-hmm." Steven tipped his head back and vaguely noted that one of the numbers on the lighted panel was out.

"Maybe we could stop off at the moon while we're at it."

"Yeah."

"Good Lord, b'y', what the hell is with you? This project has been top priority for over a year now, and you can't even muster up a little excitement over its success. Are you sick?" demanded his partner.

"No. I'm fine. What's with the mumble-jumble about a Saturn?" He frowned in bewilderment. Concentration was a hard-won feat when actively stewing over a woman. Especially when she was moaning softly into your mouth one minute and in the next was not so much as taking your phone calls.

"The planet, Kincaid, not the car."

The doors slid open, and the two men alighted, one wearing a concerned yet baffled expression and the other — well, just baffled.

"Is your neighbour still keeping you up nights?"

"Uh-huh." Steven walked into the office and tossed his briefcase on his desk before dropping listlessly into a chair. Meg hadn't returned his calls or answered her door in two days. He knew she was in there, had even heard her talking with Olaf and a woman he presumed was another friend as she saw them out last night. Unfortunately, she'd whittled down her parting remarks so that when he'd raced for the door to catch her, the only human forms on the porch were her visitors. Olaf had smiled in understanding and introduced Fannie, his girlfriend, who had likewise eyed him with compassion.

Life was cruel.

"I'd have thought her moving-in noise would have subsided by now." Jonas stood with his hands on his hips and glowered across the desk. "Why don't you complain to the landlord?"

"Oh, no. She's quieter now." *Too quiet.* Rubbing a hand along his jaw, he considered the drizzly day through the window. That was how he felt, cold and miserable. Meg was deliberately cutting him off, refusing to give him a sliver of her time. He knew she was attracted by the way she'd reacted to him, quivering at the touch of his lips on hers. What he didn't comprehend was why she insisted on fighting it so hard.

"Steven?"

"Hmm?"

"I said," Jonas repeated loudly, "why don't you join Viv and I for supper?"

Snapping out of his trance, he sat up and gave the other man his undivided attention. "Sorry. Thanks, but I've got a pile of paperwork to do."

"And a lot on your mind."

Steven shrugged. "The neighbor is giving me problems, but not the sort I can complain to Rupert about."

Jonas folded his large frame into a chair. "Tell Uncle all about it then."

"Nope."

"Ma Janey called Viv yesterday. She and Jon are planning a trip here soon."

"Don't tell me."

"Could your neighbor and the new mystery woman in your life be one and the same? I didn't make the connection when that Swedish guy called the other day asking about you. What was his name?"

"Olaf. He's a friend of hers—big brother type. Very protective." Steven glared. "References from you and my own mother aren't good enough to convince her I'm trustworthy."

Jonas chuckled slyly. "A selective woman. What's her name?"

"That would be *stubborn* woman, and her name is Meg Layton. She's a cartoonist." He'd hunted down every magazine he could with her spots in them. She was good. Really good. "And a flaming redhead—temper and all."

"I knew you were hiding a lick of good taste somewhere," his friend remarked, stroking his own fiery mustache.

"Fat lot of good it does me. I'm beginning to think she's a lost cause." The idea was uncomfortably depressing, but if she didn't want his company that was her prerogative. He wouldn't keep banging his head against that particular brick wall. Squaring his shoulders, he enquired, "What time did you say you were having supper?"

The phone interrupted Meg's fitful doze. Reaching blindly over the end of the couch, she grabbed the receiver just in time to prevent another jarring ring. The last two nights had been the absolute worst of her life, and she was grateful for a nap whenever she could get it. To be so thoroughly roused from her much-needed sleep by the rudest invention on the planet was aggravating to say the least. So, it took her a minute to assimilate who the caller was and what she was saying.

"Mother?" she slurred, stunned that it was the voice of the cultured, poised woman she used to admire as a child. What had it been? Ten years? Definitely longer than the last time she'd had any contact with her father.

"Megan Lee, where have you been hiding? Harry and I have been positively fearful that something had happened to you."

The cooing tones were another shock to Meg, who was sure that the older bleached-blonde rarely gave a thought to the daughter she'd all but abandoned.

"Where are you calling from, Alice?" The fog was lifting as she struggled to a sitting position on the couch.

"I'm with your father, of course."

"Of course. Why?"

"Darling, we *are* your family."

Alice's words sliced through her like a thousand tiny swords. She wanted something, was Meg's one coherent hypothesis. Her mother hadn't bothered with even a birthday card in ages, and now she was gushing as sweet as a banana split. Oh yeah, surmised Meg, she wanted something.

"Harry and I are going to hop the first available flight to St. John's and come visit our little girl. You've no idea how difficult it was to find you."

"Arthur Muldoon has had all my addresses since I came here," Meg dryly stated, referring to the family attorney who looked after her grandfather's estate and, consequently, her trust fund.

"Well, dear, you know how ornery and taciturn that old coot can be."

"Right." Old Arthur was one of the most agreeable characters Meg had ever known. "I'm fine, Alice. All safe and sound here in Newfoundland."

"Harry and I are worried, honeykins. You won't mind if we stay with you for a week or so, will you?"

The whiny plea abraded Meg's nerves like sandpaper.

"If you're going to be in town, you'll have to stay at a hotel. I don't have room." What she didn't say was that she couldn't stand to endure both her parents, who were practically strangers, in the same place for that long. They'd fought constantly when they'd been married, driving her to tears more times than she could count. Why had they teamed up again now? She was doubtful it was in shared disquiet over her whereabouts.

There was a pause, as if Alice couldn't quite grasp the fact that her daughter might be reluctant to see her. "Megan, we know we haven't exactly been model parents, but we'd like to begin making up for that. The detective we hired said you recently moved in to a lovely home. I'm sure you can make room for us."

"It isn't very big—and I have a roommate." Meg groaned silently, hoping she wouldn't get caught in the lie. "He's got a lot of stuff."

"Oh . . . well . . . in that case, your father and I will have to make other arrangements." Alice did *put upon* extremely well, right down to the long, drawn-out sigh. "We'll call you when we get to the airport. You can pick us up, can't you?"

"My car is in the shop." That much was true. Now all she had to do was find a roommate.

"What did you say?" Steven gawked in disbelief at the woman perched on the top step. He'd pulled into the driveway after spending a lengthy evening with the Mackenzies to find her waiting. "What kind of game are you playing? You shun me for days and then decide you might like my companionship after all. What am I missing?"

Meg's shoulders lifted in the semi-darkness. "If you really need a place to stay — "

"I don't anymore. Viv and Jonas live in a very, very, very large house. They offered to let me stay while I'm displaced from mine."

"But isn't it more convenient if you only have to move your things over here?"

Suspicion had him squinting up at her. He'd ruthlessly shoved the images he carried of her to the furthest recesses of his mind for a few scant hours only to have her pop up and jolt his awareness all over again. "What's up, Meggie?"

"Nothing."

"Nothing, huh?"

She shook her head vigorously, her glorious hair swirling around her face.

Steven sat beside her and studied the blush on her delicate cheeks. "I think you're lying."

Silence.

"If you can look me in the eye and tell me nothing's going on . . . I'll believe you."

Meg's eyes shifted to his and away.

"Right. Now, why is it that you suddenly want me at your place?" He figured it had to be serious in order for her to willingly have him move in.

"My parents are coming."

"So?"

She huffed at a curl. "So, I sort of told Alice that she and

Harry couldn't bunk with me because I have a roommate."

"Alice and Harry. You don't call them Mom and Dad?" he asked curiously.

"They never liked that. Sometimes I'd slip but—look, it's not important, okay?"

He recognized nonsense when he heard it, and that statement was definitely bullshit. What kind of weird relations did she have?

"I told you we don't have anything in common. In fact, I haven't seen either of them in years. So, when Alice called out of the blue and announced they wanted to come see me, I remembered all the fights and arguments and I panicked. I told her I had no room and figured that would sufficiently discourage her."

"But it didn't."

"No. They must want something to band together like this. Neither of them has ever shown much of an interest in me." Meg's voice was thick with dejection and suppressed anger. "Anyway, they're coming to St. John's, and I have to keep them out of my house. Otherwise, I'll never have a moment's peace."

"You said they were banding together—"

"They divorced when I was ten. The story goes, they were forced to marry because Alice got pregnant. There have been a succession of spouses for both of them."

Light was beginning to dawn for Steven. This strained situation with her parents explained some of her reticence where he was concerned. She'd witnessed a string of broken marriages and had been made to feel that her very existence was the reason for everyone's unhappiness. How could anyone raised under those circumstances trust in unconditional affection or love? How could he expect her to freely accept him into her life knowing how she'd been neglected? And how could her parents have placed the burden of their prob-

54

lems on her childish shoulders? He raged at their harsh disregard filling him.

"I don't want to relate the gory details, Steven." Meg looked tired suddenly. "If you don't want to help me, I'll understand. But if you do this one thing for me I'll be forever in your debt."

"That sounds intriguing," he quipped, trying to coax a smile from her. "How will you repay me?"

"I'll cook, clean, do your laundry, you name it."

"I'm a rotten cook, so you'll be saving yourself there. We'll just have to see what the damage is when the month is up." He twirled a ringlet around his finger and tugged playfully, at last winning a tiny grin. "Wait until your parents meet the future son-in-law from Hell."

"Oh, I didn't tell them we were involved."

"Meggie, Meggie. What else would a person think in this day and age if a woman is living with a man?"

She suggested impishly, "You could be gay."

Steven laughed heartily. "I couldn't pull that off while in the same room as you. They'd know the truth in a flash. Besides, they probably won't spend much time at your place when they see how cramped it is."

"I did say you had a load of junk."

"I do. Artsy junk."

"Let's not go overboard. I want to be able to find the front door and the bathroom still." She was smiling openly now, her eyes alight with humour.

Steven's breath caught unexpectedly. She didn't seem to notice.

"Tomorrow is Saturday. I'll bring my things over then." He stood and held out a hand for her.

She took it and rose gracefully, still grinning as she went inside.

CHAPTER FOUR

"What *is* that?" Meg quizzed as she eyed the ceramic lump furtively.

Steven set the bluish blob on the kitchen table proudly. "It's my one and only attempt at creating my own candy dish." It was only slightly larger than his fist and resembled — well, it didn't resemble anything, really. It was just a lumpy blue thing.

"Where do you put the candy? I don't see a hole."

"There isn't one. As I said, it's my only *attempt*." He tilted his head to one side and contemplated it. "I squished the bumps in just the right place for a paperweight. That was fortunate. I would have hated to throw it out."

"It appears you don't like to toss much of anything," she observed as he lifted another unidentifiable mass from the cardboard box he'd carted in. "What's that?"

"This," he proclaimed, holding the orange disc-like thing aloft, "is my one and only attempt at making an ashtray. It was lucky for me that when I dropped the clay, it smoothed out perfectly on the bottom. It doesn't tip over." He placed it next to the blob and admired it.

"Another paperweight?" It was tough not to laugh at his earnest demeanor.

"No, it's a candy dish."

Meg giggled. She couldn't help it.

For the last two hours, Steven had been running in and out of her apartment with one odd item after another. His hockey gear from college, a hot-pink coffee percolator, his first pair of sunglasses — the ones that his girlfriend in high school told him looked cool — a picture of a very famous computer mogul with his pants around his knees and a drunken grin on his face — insurance, he'd said, in case he ever had to butt heads with the man.

Uncertain whether to be charmed or appalled that he kept practically *everything*, Meg could only stand back and watch whilst he turned her home into a pack rat's paradise.

Most of his things fit into the spare room. His computer system and desk had replaced her drawing table, and his television rested above the foot of his bed. He'd hauled his clothing in and thrown it across the bed for now, vowing to straighten it all out as soon as he retrieved the necessary knickknacks to make his stay seem *authentic* to her parents.

A freight train didn't expend as much energy as Steven Kincaid on a mission.

"I think that about does it." His brow furrowed in concentration, he tapped a sneakered foot and scratched his chest. The Geeks Do It Most Thoroughly slogan on his ragged T-shirt was incongruous on his muscled frame when it stretched taut over those breathtakingly broad shoulders.

Meg shut off her rambling thoughts abruptly, mentally stepping on her hormones. When had the simple act of a man scratching his chest stimulated her this much? Or at all, for that matter?

"When are your parents due in?" Steven asked a second time.

"Oh, ah . . . around four. I booked them at a swanky hotel and arranged to have someone meet them. That's what they used to prefer. I doubt if they've changed much in that regard." Effusive hugs and kisses at the airport gate had never appealed to Alice and Harry.

"They like to travel in style, huh?" He was staring at her closely, making her feel like he could decipher every frown and twitch that crossed her face.

She shrugged, suddenly uncomfortable. "They like the extra attention."

"Where will I put Bazil?" The question was so unexpected that it took a few moments to sink in.

"You don't have a Bazil."

Steven coughed. "Actually, since I've always felt rotten about lying—and since the whole purpose of my moving in here is to *discourage* your parents from hanging around, I figured a pet might go nicely."

"You didn't go out and get a cockatoo," Meg said disbelievingly. "That's just—you *did*?"

"He's on loan."

"What?"

"I really wasn't sure about taking him home, so the store owner said to try him out for a few days. If I don't like him I can take him back." Apparently, this made sense to Steven, who only days ago was complaining about his nonexistent parrot's stress level.

"You'll ruin him that way," she scolded, "bringing him home and taking him back. The bird will be confused and high-strung."

Heaving a sigh, he agreed. "I realized that as soon as I got him in the car. Now I'll have to keep him. That means carrying him over here."

"You are such a strange man."

"But I'm adorable." He leaned toward her. "We should practice kissing."

Meg snorted. "I'm not telling Alice and Harry we're involved and that's final. There's no need for us to practice."

"I meant for my benefit. It's been ages since I kissed anyone."

"It was three days ago . . . on my porch . . . in front of Johnny."

"That kid has rotten timing."

Planting a firm hand in the middle of his chest, she held him off. "No passes of any kind. This is going to be a platonic arrangement."

"You'll be sorry."

"I doubt it," she lied.

"I'll be sorry for both of us." He snapped his fingers as if remembering something and moved into the living room. There he stood, surveying the area with a serious gaze. "Could we shove your drawing table over a little? It's right where my recliner needs to go."

"What do you mean?" Meg sidled up to him and looked from her work space to the television. The table was in direct line with the set but, as she then explained to her house-guest, was situated to best avail of the natural light coming in through the window. "I'm not moving it. You'll have to stay in your room and watch TV."

Hands on his hips, he scowled off into space and muttered, "And to think that I agreed to do you such a huge favor. A man's most comfortable possession is his easy chair. Would you deprive me of it so callously?"

"No, you're right. Seeing as how it's your dearest piece of furniture—we'll just have to put the bed back in your apartment and then you can sleep in the chair."

"Okay."

Meg looked at him derisively. "You would actually sleep in it?"

"Only if I doze during commercials. That has happened once or twice. I could sleep in your bed," he suggested hopefully.

"There's just one tiny problem."

"What's that?"

"*I'm* sleeping in my bed." She glared at his grinning face and enunciated, "Alone."

"You're no fun."

Steven loved baiting her. Every time he made a remark that was even remotely suggestive, she got all flushed and prickly. She was beautiful.

Bazil, the salmon-crested cockatoo, was a hit with Meg. She *oohed* over the preening bird for a long time when he brought the cage in and set it on a table near the open window. She protested that the enclosure was too small for such a magnificent creature, hauling out the phone book to scan for the number to a pet supply shop where she could purchase a larger one.

Baz stared out over his curved beak at the humans. He walked haughtily from one end of his perch to the other, curiously examining his new surroundings.

Steven thought he might be hungry, so he unlatched the cage and placed a few nuts inside. Baz bent to one side and looked as if he were about to fall from the perch. Then, ignoring the food given so freely, he boldly stepped through the door and onto the table.

"You can't come out here," Steven told him. "Go back." He tried shooing the bird this way and that, gently pushing as Baz calmly avoided direction. He didn't jump or squawk excitedly, just strutted around the table top in a leisurely fashion.

"I don't think we need to worry about his stressed-out disposition for now," Meg observed. She leaned down to Baz's level. "You can stay out, but don't poop on the furniture."

"Meg, he's an animal. He doesn't understand you."

Baz pushed his head forward and rubbed his pecker against Meg's nose very carefully.

"How sweet! Steven, did you see that?" She laughed delightedly and rubbed back.

"Mmph. I can do that." He'd never have believed he could be jealous of a dumb bird.

"It's not cute if you do it."

Sighing, he repeated, "Baz doesn't understand about keeping the place clean. We can't let him run amok."

Meg went to the broom closet and dug around inside. She emerged with yesterday's newspaper and proceeded to put it in the far corner of the room where it was barely noticeable.

Baz, who had been watching his new mistress with great interest, obligingly flew to the paper. There, he did his business without a qualm and waddled around the kitchen loftily to further explore the environment.

"See? He's housebroken." Meg beamed at their pet, enamored. "He's gorgeous, isn't he?"

"Yeah," Steven grunted. "Splendid." All he kept thinking was what a rotten idea it was to bring a pet home. Now her attention would be riveted elsewhere. That wouldn't do. "Maybe it's not a good thing to have him here. I mean, I'm at work all day, and you're busy. What if he's lonely?"

"I work at home. I can talk to him while I sketch." Her baby blues followed Baz when he hopped onto a chair. "He'll be wonderful company."

"I'll leave the door to his cage open. His food's in there."

She nodded, smiling. "I'm glad you brought him home." Affectionately, she kissed his cheek.

Steven forgot that he was peeved and offered the interloper a fig. Slowly, the illegal tenant accepted what he obviously considered his due and screeched something the humans assumed was a grudging *thank you*.

"Darling!" Alice gushed and drifted across the hotel room.

Bestowing an air kiss next to Meg's cheek, she tipped her stylishly coiffured head to one side and studied her. She blinked as if to dispel a motherly tear even though her eyes were dry. "Look how you've grown. Harry, isn't she beautiful?"

Her father hadn't bothered to rise from his reclining position on the sofa. He waved a hand behind his graying head in a half-hearted salute and continued to watch the soap opera on the big-screen TV.

"Come sit down, Megan. We've been soooooo worried about you." Alice grasped her daughter's limp hands and led her to a chair, which was just as well considering Meg was having a hard time getting her feet to move.

The niggling notion that something was up returned full force while Alice chattered and even condescended to pour tea for two. Her father was nursing a drink—probably not his first—as he chewed rapidly on a scone.

Meg tried to focus on what her mother was saying, but the whole scenario seemed ridiculous to her. Alice and Harry, who hadn't changed a bit, were together on a trip to visit their forgotten offspring. This behavior was unprecedented and, therefore, not to be trusted. Yet, some small part of Meg wanted to believe that they really had worried, that they had come across the St. Lawrence strait just to make sure she was okay.

Yeah, right!

A moment passed before she realized that Alice had stopped talking and was waiting expectantly for an answer. "Well, dear? Do we get to meet your roommate? He sounded absolutely yummy on the phone." The older woman's eyes fairly sparkled at the mention of an attractive male.

Some things never change one iota. Meg wished that Steven hadn't ignored her warning and struck up a lively conversation when the call had come announcing her parents' arrival. He'd been his usual charming self and had dropped blatant hints that he and Meg were a couple. So blatant, in fact, that she knew it would be useless to tell her mother otherwise.

"Oh, I doubt it, Alice. Steven's not quite himself since — well, since the breakdown." She bit her lip hard and prayed God wouldn't punish her too severely for the lie. It was the only way she could think of to deter her mother's prying.

"He's been ill?" Alice had never functioned in a socially rounded way and was fearful of anyone who might be determined as *different* by her standards.

Meg counted on it.

"No, not exactly. It's difficult to explain."

"I see. Well, perhaps a little *hello* would suffice."

"Yes, he has no problem with people over the phone. It's the personal interaction he can't deal with." Meg crossed her fingers beneath her purse, hoping the fires of Hell weren't burning hotter for her benefit. Anxious to change the subject, she asked, "How's the hotel service?" and let Alice ramble on with the routine litany of complaints ranging from bad food — the hotel had a five-star chef — to an understocked bar — her mother *had* to have four olives per martini. Everything else was trivial.

"We're hoping to spend some quality time with you, Megan. It's been so long since we really talked."

Meg looked blankly at her concerned expression. She and her parents had never *really talked*. They'd disregarded every overture she'd made as a child and then as a teenager. Why had they shown up years after she'd accepted that she didn't matter to them and decided to cut her losses? She'd known then that Alice and Harry were of that breed who ought not to have children for one reason or another.

Pursing her thin lips at the lack of response from Meg, her mother said, "I can tell you're surprised and our visit is a bit much to take in. Why don't we have lunch tomorrow? Then Harry and I can meet your Steven and see your house. It won't upset him, will it?"

"I don't know if he'll be home. He may have to go to wo — ah, therapy."

Alice shrugged. "That's fine. We'll come by around one."

Harry absently tossed a farewell over his shoulder as Meg left.

The ride home in her three-year-old coupe seemed like a blur when she replayed the conversation with Alice. Traffic was at a crawl, every light red, and she tapped her fingers impatiently on the wheel.

When she eventually dragged her tense body from the car, she was too confused to see straight. With each heavy step toward her door, she wondered again what her parents were up to.

"Baz!" Steven peeked into Meg's bedroom and found it empty. "Baz!" he yelled a bit louder, growing more panicked by the second. The bird had wandered off while he was talking to his mother on the phone and was nowhere to be seen. He'd checked every room in the apartment twice. No Baz.

Spying the open kitchen window, he groaned. Surely the white fiend hadn't gone AWOL less than twenty-four hours in his new abode. Or had he?

Steven stuck his head through the gap and looked left. Then right. Up. Down.

No Baz.

Meg would kill him. She loved that bird, had taken to him like a mother hen. Or in this case, mother cockatoo.

"Bazil?" he called tentatively.

A shriek startled him into clutching his chest, and the animal in question dropped down on the sill. He eyed the man enquiringly, as if he didn't know he'd been lost.

"So, that's it, huh? If I ask for you, you'll come. If I demand, you hide."

Baz dipped his regal head once.

"All right, buddy. But let's keep this frantic episode between us. Meg is preoccupied enough as it is." He carefully urged the cockatoo onto his hand and transferred him to a shoulder.

Baz liked an elevated position.

The front door slamming behind her, Meg entered the kitchen with a flushed face and hair swirling. The rigid set of her jaw told Steven the meeting with her parents had gone as badly as she'd anticipated. Without sparing either him or his bird a glance, she stalked through the house and into her room. That door was also abused with much force, the bang reverberating so strongly that the pots hanging from the kitchen ceiling swayed in response.

Baz nudged his perch's ear and tipped his head in question.

Shrugging his birdless shoulder, Steven muttered, "Rough day, I guess."

Baz agreed—sort of.

Once he'd found something for the *pet* to busy himself with—namely food—he tapped hesitantly on Meg's door. "Hey, aren't you gonna tell me how it went? Meg?"

The door was thrust wide, and she stood nose to nose with him, even though she had to crane her neck to achieve such a feat. Her eyes glittered as she wordlessly poked him in the chest three times.

"What was that for?" he demanded. "I haven't done anything wrong!"

"Alice wants to meet you. Despite the fact that I tried desperately to discourage her, both she and Harry are coming for lunch tomorrow." Meg glared at him and inhaled deeply in what he assumed was an effort to lower her blood pressure. "I told them you'd had some kind of breakdown, so you'd better behave that way if you happen to be around when they get here."

"Why would you tell them that?" he asked, confounded. "I'm perfectly balanced."

"It freaks Alice out. But they're coming anyway."

"Good."

"*Good*?" Her brow wrinkled cutely.

"Yep. I want to meet them." Maybe then he could understand what sort of deranged people could forget they had such a lovely, talented woman for a daughter. "Why don't you come out to the kitchen and I'll make some tea? You can tell me all about it."

Fifteen minutes later, he had a pretty good idea how the dialogue between Meg and her parents—or rather, just Alice—had gone.

"Why are you so certain they're up to something, Meg? Maybe they're genuinely sorry for the way they neglected you."

"Look, my father barely acknowledged I was in the room. That was no surprise. What floored me was that he was there at all. And Alice is far too adept at putting on a show for me to decide if she was serious." Meg closed her eyes and rubbed a hand across them tiredly. "I didn't even think to ask why they were together. Last I heard, they couldn't stand the sight of one another."

Steven walked behind her chair and kneaded the muscles of her neck and shoulders. After her initial resistance, she let her head droop forward docilely, exposing her nape to his tender ministrations. He focused on getting her to relax and fought the heat that radiated from his fingertips to the rest of his body.

Meg moaned submissively, leaning back into the massage and arching her slender neck. His hands went, of their own volition, to cup the underside of her jaw, easing the tension gradually. He slid them higher, into her hair, and gently rubbed her scalp and then her temples. The helpless sound she made sent desire shooting to his groin like a flash fire, igniting the passion he'd tried to suppress but failed.

"Better?" Steven whispered, valiantly shoving his salacious feelings aside. This wasn't the time to be plotting her seduction. Meg needed his support and comfort, not for his selfish libido to kick into overdrive.

"Mmm-hmm. Thanks." Her hands covered his where they rested now on her shoulders. "You don't have to be here for lunch tomorrow. It's probably best anyway. I can't expect you to coddle me for the duration of the family visit."

"I wouldn't mind." He placed a kiss on her soft hair and mumbled, "If it's coddling you need, I could always extend my services beyond their departure."

She laughed quietly. "I must say, having a houseguest isn't as bad as I thought. I guess I'm just so accustomed to living alone."

"Why is that?" He combed his fingers through her hair soothingly, loving the silky feel of it.

"I dunno."

Steven suspected that she'd been alone too long and that while she might be used to it, she didn't particularly care for it. He hoped he could convince her to let him invade her space on a permanent basis.

"I think you only like me for my bird." He grinned when she chuckled, reveling in the husky vibrations. The woman's laugh was adorably sexy — like the rest of her.

"Where is Baz?"

"Who?"

"The bird," she reminded him.

"Oh, *that* bird."

Meg slapped his hand. "You're awful."

"I'm naughty, yes, if that's what you mean." He slipped

his arms around her snugly and lightly pecked her cheek. Encouraged when she nuzzled him hesitantly, he moved his mouth to hers. Deliberately, he kept the embrace brief, the cautious sweep of his lips a mere tease in comparison to what he craved. But he'd made her jittery before, and the need to have her close emotionally outweighed his desire in importance. So, he released her a second later and congratulated himself on his restraint.

Meg cast a surreptitious glance Steven's way as he set the table. He'd mastered the art after only one lesson and was studiously working on his serving abilities. She'd gladly accepted responsibility for the cooking after he told her how he and JJ had nearly burned Jonas out of his apartment in college while attempting to bake a casserole. House fires she didn't need.

Cooking and baking were not a chore for her. Growing up, she was forbidden to enter the kitchen or sign up for Home Ec classes. It was above the Laytons to look so domestic — that was what *help* was for. So, when she'd struck out on her own, she went a tiny bit ape at the supermarkets and department stores. She had to feed herself anyway. A well-stocked cupboard and the tools to putter about with had given her a sense of independence.

She was still puzzled that only hours ago he'd given up the ideal opportunity to make a serious pass and had left her cold instead. Hadn't her moment of weakness been what he was waiting for? Or had he been turned off by her obvious reaction? Maybe he was only interested in the chase. That was the explanation foremost in her mind — he probably wouldn't have given her a second look if she'd been more susceptible to his charms in the first place.

On the other hand, she could have sworn she'd tasted the

same passion on his lips that had raged through her traitorously before he'd pulled back. His face was slightly flushed, those green eyes as dark as a turbulent sea. He'd definitely looked aroused.

Meg stirred the heating pasta sauce and sighed. How would she recognize passion when she saw it? She was an untouched virgin. Well, mostly untouched . . . if you didn't count those few mindless minutes when Steven had kissed the daylights out of her right in this very room—on the countertop, no less.

Lifting her hair off a neck that was very hot, she fanned her skin rapidly.

"I think you should move away from the stove, Meggie. You look a little too—"

"I'm fine," she snapped at the confusing man who'd claimed he wanted her. What was she thinking? Her own parents had never wanted her. Why would he?

Steven whistled lowly. "You're in a mood. I hope you're not still worrying about Agnes and Humphrey."

"Alice and Harry," she corrected, the unexpected sting of tears pricking. What was wrong with her, she wondered a bit wildly, that no one could love her? Was she too thin, too ugly, too fat, too strange? What had she been born with that tainted her so that she turned out to be someone that even a mother couldn't take to?

"Meg?"

"What?" she sniffled.

"Tell me what's wrong." Steven reached around her to shut off the burner and remove the saucepan. He turned her to face him and tipped her chin up, not letting her hide from his knowing gaze.

"It's nothing," Meg denied.

"You don't strike me as the type to spring a leak for no reason." He folded her close and tucked her head against his chest. "I only want to help. Don't cry, love."

Meg wrapped her arms around him and let him rock her consolingly, the steady rhythm of his heart keeping time in her ear. She would not tell him that his earlier withdrawal had hurt her deeply or that the one person she longed to hold on to was him. She was not a crybaby or a wimp. She didn't need him, she told herself even as she squeezed him tighter. She'd never needed anyone.

"I'm sorry. I get weepy this time of the month." One more hug was all she wanted. "You can let go now."

"Whenever you're ready."

"Oh." Maybe a minute more. "Okay."

"Meggie?"

"Hmm?"

"Sweetheart, if you don't move, I can't be held responsible for what happens next."

Then, for the first time, she became aware of the rigid bulge pressing into her belly. He was totally, hugely aroused.

Meg wiggled a little, testing him.

A strangled groan escaped his throat.

She smiled, feeling vindicated. "I'm sorry about that, too."

"Sure, you minx. If you weren't so vulnerable right now, I'd see how sorry you are."

"Is that why you stopped kissing me before?" she enquired, raising her head.

The pained expression on his face was proof enough. He quirked a thick eyebrow, and she giggled. "Be careful. I don't think you realize what you do to me. Now, feed me or I'll forget what a noble guy I am."

Baz chose that moment to remind the humans that he was due some attention and deigned to reclaim his perch on Steven's shoulder. He looked at Meg sideways and changed his mind about the position he'd chosen, carefully stepping down on her red head.

"He won't fall from there, will he?" she queried, grinning.

"Nah. He jumped on me like that this morning. His claws aren't hurting you?" Steven lifted a hand to stroke her cheek tenderly.

"No."

"Good." He petted Baz's puffed chest awkwardly. "Behave," he warned the bird.

Baz scowled.

Meg finished preparing dinner with a feathery hat on.

That night, she lay in bed and remembered the surge of satisfaction she'd felt to discover the effect she had on him. He hadn't been turned off by her but had respected her enough to give her some room. The problem now was she didn't know if she wanted any space at all.

She stopped kidding herself that she wasn't tempted. Not that she needed him, she repeated mentally for the hundredth time. He was a virile, attractive, available man. She wanted to know what it was like to make love with him, to be one with him.

If she went to his room and slipped beneath the covers, would he insist she was vulnerable and didn't know what she was doing? Perhaps, if she was lucky, he'd be half asleep and unable to think rationally.

Meg discarded that line of thought. It smacked of manipulation and deceit. She'd always felt disdain for women who tried that sort of thing. If she and Steven were to become lovers, she wanted there to be no games between them.

Meg was positive she could have an affair with him and thoroughly enjoy herself. Marriage was still out, but she didn't think he wanted to get that serious anyhow. After all, any man worth his salt could see that she wasn't made from family material, and Steven was a smart one.

Content that she'd straightened her emotions out, she

rolled onto her side and snuggled down for the night. Her roommate would be there in the morning.

Steven grinned in the darkness. He was confident Meg was coming around. Little by little, she was beginning to trust him. Hopefully, she would open herself up to the possibility of a relationship with him. A long-term relationship—life-long.

He was ruined. All those cracks he'd made to his friends about stepping onto the matrimonial bandwagon echoed in his mind. He'd been kidding, of course. The women Jonas and JJ had chosen to spend their lives with were ideal mates for them. He was simply envious of their happiness and didn't want them feeling sorry for him.

Laughing to himself, he recalled wearing black from head to toe only months ago when JJ had moved in with his then-fiancée and her two boys. He'd lamented the loss of another good man and helped arrange his furniture. JJ had just shaken his head and cautioned that his time was coming.

It *was* about time, too. Steven was more than ready to start a family. That the woman of his dreams had practically dropped in his lap was pure luck.

Visions of tiny toddlers with Meg's hair and his eyes had taken over his brain.

A thump in the other room had his muscles tensing. Was she having as much trouble sleeping as he was?

The sound of her door opening had him sitting upright in bed. He cocked an ear and waited for another noise to indicate what she was doing.

Water running in the kitchen had him at his own door. Meg was passing it on the way back to her room and stopped instantly when she noticed him.

"Hi. Did I wake you?" Her whispery voice sent a shiver

up his bare back.

"I couldn't sleep anyway. You okay?"

She nodded, the dimly lit hallway stealing his chance to read her expression. "Just restless."

"Anything I can do?" Steven wondered if she knew how delectable she was in that voluminous night shirt. He itched to peel it off her.

Meg was silent for a while, as if considering his question. "No, not tonight."

"Tomorrow night?"

"We'll see." She drifted past him and closed her door softly.

That was a definite improvement. He willed his nuisance of an erection to disappear. Not right now, but maybe tomorrow.

We'll see.

"You bet your sweet petunias, Ms. Layton."

A feeble squawk from the kitchen told him to give it a rest.

CHAPTER FIVE

Meg checked her reflection in the hallway mirror as she went to let Alice and Harry in. The outfit she'd chosen was one of the few things in her closet that looked professional. She'd bought it for a meeting with a magazine editor who'd been interested in her spots and had worn it just that once. The black pantsuit made her feel confident and in control, so it was perfect for today's lunch. She had no intention of letting her parents see how nervous she really was to have them in her home.

Steven had offered to stay and give her moral support, but she'd managed to persuade him to go to the office. She'd thanked him profusely for his concern as he got in his car and then again when he'd called between appointments to see how her morning was going. He'd known she was battling to keep her frayed nerves from disintegrating altogether. Meg wasn't accustomed to having anyone bother about her feelings, and she was touched. So touched that her throat had ached suspiciously, and she'd hurried off the phone before he noticed the wobble in her voice.

Now, the table was set with her best linen and china, the napkins folded precisely. Every utensil had been buffed to a shine, and the crystal glasses sparkled.

The salad was cold, the rolls were hot, and the main dish of cubed ham and peppered omelets was warming pleasantly in the oven.

Baz had objected stridently to being confined to his cage, and Meg felt terrible for that. Unfortunately, she knew that if she left him out, he'd likely stroll over Alice's toes and cause a panic.

Alice disliked animals and about ninety percent of the entire human population. The rest she could bend to her will.

Meg drew a fortifying breath and welcomed the older couple inside. After seating them in the now crowded living room, she went to check on the food. Just as she was uncorking the wine, the phone rang.

"Are you sure you don't want me there?" Steven demanded when she answered.

"It's fine, really." Meg almost smiled at the frustrated sound he made. "If I need you I'll call."

"All right. I'll just wait out here then."

"Pardon?"

"In the driveway."

Shoving the curtains aside, she peered through the window. Steven waved from his car, the cell phone wedged between his chin and shoulder as he huddled comfortably behind the wheel.

"Are you crazy?" she growled.

"I'm supposed to be, remember?"

Meg shook her head dazedly. "You don't have to sit out there. You may as well come in."

"No, I think it would serve you best if I stayed where I am."

"What about lunch? You have to eat something."

"I have a sandwich. Lettuce and cheese." He heaved a great sigh. "I also have a banana." He held that up for inspection.

"I'll bring you some lunch."

"Oh, would you?" crooned the man Meg was convinced was certifiable. But he was a sweet nut and was waiting in his car if she wanted to crook a finger. That was endearing.

"I'll sneak you an omelet," she promised.

"I'd be grateful."

When she went back to the living room, Alice was examining the large watercolor above the couch. It was one of Meg's, a serene picture of a field of wild flowers and children frolicking.

"This is cute, Megan. Did you paint it? Look, Harry," she instructed without pausing to hear a response.

"It's mine," Meg confirmed.

Harry stared at the scene morosely and remarked, "Mmm. A bit generic for my taste."

"Lunch is ready." One more gushing compliment from her father and she might titter with delight. Better to move on to the food. That was one of the rare things Harry showed interest in—right behind a drink, pretty women, and money.

The meal was consumed in silence, broken only by the scraping of Harry's fork while he made quick work of both food and wine.

Meg excused herself and assembled Steven's lunch, chattering nonstop about her elderly neighbor whom she often cooked for. "I'll just run over with this and be right back." The front door slammed behind her, and she breathed a sigh of relief. The atmosphere in the kitchen was so tense it was a wonder nobody popped a vessel.

"Everything okay?" Steven took the covered plate and mug of hot coffee through his window and set them on the passenger seat. "You look whacked."

"I'm just hoping they won't stay long. I have to get back before they wonder what I'm doing."

"Too late." His eyebrows rose, and he tipped his head toward the apartment. "I believe your mother got curious."

She groaned painfully and avoided looking up at the window. "I guess she's seen you."

Steven grinned and patted her hand. "Tell her the truth.

That I'm out here and don't want to come in."

"You're dying to go in there and ham it up," she stated shakily.

"Not until I've finished eating. I plan to enjoy lunch before setting foot inside. They might ruin my digestion."

Alice was back at the table when Meg returned, the grim line of her mouth and Harry's a sure sign they'd been arguing.

"Was that your young man out there, dear?" Her mother's frown had cleared the instant Meg closed the door.

"Um, yes."

"Is he coming in?"

"Maybe later. I told you he's a bit, ah, antisocial?" The blush creeping up her neck was more embarrassing than the conversation. "He's going to eat in the car."

Harry's stretch of civility had apparently reached its limit as he loudly postulated, "What sort of weirdo are you tangled up with, girl? Certainly, a Layton can do better than to attach herself to some freak."

"Harry," Alice scolded, seemingly affronted. "Ignore your father, Megan. He doesn't know what he's saying." She glared a silent warning at him and turned on a smile. "It would be presumptuous of us to intrude on your private life, darling."

Meg, stung by her father's words, muttered, "Amen to that."

Harry harrumphed and gulped the last of the wine.

An earsplitting shriek frightened Alice into spilling her coffee, and Meg smiled a little, thankful for the interruption.

"That's Baz. I think he wants to be let out of my room." She dashed to the back of the apartment and retrieved the cross bird. "Be nice, sweetheart," she told him. "They won't be here much longer."

"Good Lord, Megan. Why didn't you just get a canary or

something? That ... *thing* is enormous. Not to mention rather surly-looking." Alice couldn't shrink any farther from the cage. Her carefully made-up face crinkled in horror. "What the devil is it?"

"It's a macaw," Harry knowingly expounded. "One of those endangered types. Probably cost a fortune."

"Actually," Meg supplied, for the misnomer seemed to have irritated Bazil greatly, "it's a cockatoo. I don't think this one's on the current endangered species list."

Harry grunted, never one to appreciate having his ignorance corrected. "Who cares? The damned creatures are all nuisances."

Baz's squawk was deafening, and he flapped his wings.

"You've hurt his feeling, Harry. He understands quite a bit of English." Meg placed the cage squarely on the counter and proceeded to open the door.

The clatter of chair legs announced Alice's imminent departure, the possibility of live entertainment apparently too much for her. "We'll be off now, darling," she trilled in a querulous voice. "No need to let him out for us. I'm sure he's very intelligent."

Meg closed the cage again, thinking the ploy had worked and she was home free. She made some faint objection that they were leaving so soon and couldn't they stay a while longer, but Alice had had all the wildlife she could handle and headed for the exit with a flourish. She was brought up short, however, by a considerable six-foot-plus frame.

Steven skittered backward, as if alarmed by the sudden emergence of Meg's parents. She had to cover her mouth to halt the threatening giggles. He really was something. The mock dread on his handsome face was very convincing. Anyone who didn't know better would swear he was repelled by the sight of other humans.

Harry and Alice stepped back a pace and simply stared.

"This is Steven. Honey," Meg said in a soothing tone, "meet my parents."

"He-he-he-hello," stuttered Steven weakly, one hand swiping across his brow in a nervous gesture. It was a nice touch that he decided to forgo the handshake, his fingers trembling ineptly as he slid along the wall while tossing wide-eyed looks at the older couple. When he reached Meg, he positioned himself behind her, and she was hard pressed not to laugh at her parents' astonished expressions.

"It takes Steven some time to get used to new people."

"Oh." Alice's hand fluttered to her throat. "Lovely to meet you, Steven," she shouted.

"Yes," bellowed Harry. "We must get together soon."

"Goodbye now!" Alice added loudly, and they scuttled out the door.

Meg collapsed in a chair and laughed until her sides hurt and tears streamed down her face. She'd never seen either of her parents at such a loss for words.

"Well, I don't know what you find so funny, but frankly, I'm insulted." Steven joined her at the table and poured himself a cup of coffee. "I did my best to look paranoid, and they thought I was hard of hearing. Not very observant at all."

Wiping her eyes, Meg tried to console him. "Don't take it personally. They don't pay much attention to anyone but themselves. They never have."

"Do you think I spooked them?"

"You spooked me, and I knew what you were doing." She sobered then and mused aloud, "They haven't changed. Harry didn't even pretend he wanted to be here. I'm not sure what's up yet."

He took her hand in his and stroked his thumb over the back of it. The action was comforting and warm, making Meg feel she wasn't alone. He sincerely wanted to help.

"I'm glad you were here," she murmured, not looking at

him. It was amazing how much better she'd handled the situation just knowing he was right there in the driveway, ready to cause a diversion if necessary.

He brushed his mouth over her knuckles gently. "Don't mention it."

The air in the kitchen grew thick with anticipation. Meg watched, entranced, when he lowered his head. His green eyes were fastened on her lips, their fierce depths hypnotizing. A sigh caressed her mouth, and she couldn't tell if it was his or hers as the space between them dwindled to a fraction of an inch.

"Have you fed Baz yet today?" Steven asked all of a sudden, and her eyes enlarged confusedly.

"You want to enquire after the bird's welfare *now*?"

"Why not now?"

"Because . . . you were about to kiss me."

"You said no passes. Strictly platonic," he had the nerve to repeat stoically. "I respect you far too much too take advantage."

Meg huffed, "Go ahead, take advantage. Just this once."

"I'm shocked. How could you try to ruin a gentleman that way?"

"I won't mind."

He shook his head sadly. "If only my mother hadn't raised me so well. I'll kiss you later. When you've recovered from lunch."

"It wasn't that big an ordeal, Kincaid. Kiss me now or not at all."

"You drive a hard bargain, but I'll wait." He rose and ruffled her hair. "Feed Bazil. I can't have a desperate woman *and* a starving bird on my conscience."

"*Desperate?*" Meg blinked at his retreating figure, jaw slack. "You'll pay for that, mister!"

"So, when can we meet her?" Viv, who was conserving office space by sitting on her husband's lap, raised a dark-blonde eyebrow.

Jonas was wearing an amused look that said, *I told you so.* The family inquisition had progressed to the determined stage, the stage where nobody was satisfied simply to know that Steven had found The One. They now had to badger him mercilessly for a peek at the woman.

"Not yet. She's skittish." That was true. He would dearly love to introduce Meg to the Kincaid clan but sensed she wasn't ready. He needed a little more time to woo her, gain her trust.

Viv smoothed a hand over her swelling abdomen thoughtfully. It was a gesture he'd watched her perform often since she'd discovered she was pregnant, a nurturing motion to let the baby know she was constantly thinking of the life blooming inside her. "How skittish?" she demanded lowly. "You've been known to disturb even the most relaxed female."

Steven grimaced. "She claims she doesn't want marriage or children."

"Oh, Steven." Viv's expression communicated doubt. "I suppose you mean to convince her otherwise." This was said in such a way that suggested it was already a lost cause, an opinion that he'd shared only a couple of days ago.

"Meg doesn't realize what she wants yet," he growled.

"And there's probably a good reason for that."

"Two reasons. I've met them." He smiled grimly while he recalled their hasty departure that afternoon. "I can handle them."

Viv shared a look with her husband.

Jonas shrugged and observed, "Meg's reserve bothers the family. They think a woman who doesn't see what a prize you are needs her head examined." He had some trouble not choking on the *prize* part.

"There's nothing wrong with her head. Her folks have done a rotten number on her. I'll persuade her to win me."

Viv rolled her eyes. "Bring her to supper tomorrow."

"I'm not sure if she's free."

"Bring her to supper."

Steven virtually snarled, "Don't push."

"Jonas and I will expect you at seven."

"I'm so glad you're the one who has to deal with her now," he told his partner.

The big man chuckled. "I like the challenge."

"I'll bring Meg as long as you promise not to invite the twins. One sisterly probe is enough. I don't want her psychologically damaged over the appetizers."

"Cass and Caro might invite themselves." Viv smiled compassionately. "Don't worry. We'll be careful of her."

"Yes, you will." Steven checked his watch. "I have work to do. You remember what that is, don't you, Mackenzie? That stuff we do when our laps are empty?"

"Oh, yeah. I'm considering early retirement. This job thing interferes with my life." Jonas squeezed his wife affectionately while she nuzzled his neck. "Didn't you just say you had something to do?"

Steven breezily exhaled. "Toss a hint, why don't you? Get off him before the next meeting, Viv. People will think he's a hopelessly lovesick dud and invest their money elsewhere. The stocks will plummet. I'll lose good profit."

The newlyweds ignored him, so he left.

That night, he pretended to concentrate on paperwork while Meg sketched beneath the light of a lamp. Her face was serious as her hand flew adeptly over the drawing. Her vibrant hair shone, his fingers itching to tangle in the silky curls falling about her shoulders. He shifted restlessly on the couch.

"What is it?" Meg prompted, her attention never leaving the table. "You've been staring for a good fifteen minutes."

"Does that annoy you?"

"Greatly."

"Sorry." Steven debated whether or not to open up the can of worms but then decided he may as well prepare her. "We've been invited out tomorrow."

The busy hand stilled. "We?"

"Mmm-hmm. Jonas and Viv want us to go over to the estate." He counted the seconds of silence tensely.

"Why would they ask both of us?" Meg lifted her eyes slowly. "We're not a couple."

Uh-oh. "Well, since we are living together—"

"Temporarily."

"—and my mother assumed that we were seeing each other. I saw no reason to correct the mistake. Fortunately, if the family believes that I'm involved they won't try to set me up on any blind dates. If you'd only been there when Eleuthera's third cousin tried to seduce me—at Viv's instigation, I might add—you'd take pity and just come to dinner." His beseeching gaze fell on the swell of her breasts, barely visible above her tank top. He swallowed. "Or you could take pity and come to bed with me. The latter I prefer but I'll settle for supper."

Meg stared at him for a long time. "Why don't we just sleep together and get it over with? I don't need to meet your family for that, do I?"

That stumped him. "You want to sleep with me?"

"It'd be a waste of time denying it."

"But you don't want to meet my family," he stated redundantly.

"I don't think it's necessary when two people have an affair that they have to—"

"*An affair?*"

"That is what we're talking about." She fixed a guileless look on him.

"I don't want an affair, Meg."

"But you just said — "

"I... want... it... all." Steven's glare was explicit. "Marriage, kids, the whole shebang."

"Oh, then I guess you really will have to settle for supper. I'm not doing the rest." She went back to her sketch.

He threw down his pen and went to confer with Baz in the kitchen.

"What am I doing wrong?" he asked the majestic bird. "I'm loving and loyal, faithful and reliable... moderately attractive."

Baz blinked.

"It is not normal for a woman not to have the nesting instinct. She's out of whack. But she wants me." He jabbed a finger in the air. "I can work with that."

Meg was still drawing when he returned.

Her head came up, and she eyed him warily. "What now?"

Steven held up his arms in defeat. "We'll have an affair... after we go to the Mackenzie's."

"I don't want to meet them."

"Just once. That's the deal."

"Okay," she agreed quietly.

"Okay. We'll see about the rest."

Meg didn't respond.

Back in the kitchen, Baz objected to being deserted with a piercing squawk. Steven and Meg bumped into one another as they tried getting through the same doorway. They nudged and groped and finally freed themselves sufficiently to see to the bird. He measured them closely and seemed to decide he wasn't so lonely after all. But it was clear he wanted out of the cage, so they let him out.

"You owe me a kiss," Steven informed Meg as he tracked the cockatoo's movements around the room. He'd learned it didn't pay to let him stray too far.

"I don't owe you a thing. You didn't want to kiss me earlier, you don't need to do it now." She went to the window and closed it firmly, her own gaze on the wandering animal.

"I wanted to, but you were too uptight. It wouldn't have been good for you."

She made a disgusted sound. "You mean, for *you*."

"I would love to touch you any time, any way, any place. Let me show you." He pinned her against the wall and tipped her head back.

Her blue eyes dared him to kiss her, her mouth set mutinously.

This called for a disciplined approach.

With admirable restraint, he feathered his mouth over hers once, twice, then a third time, each teasing touch lingering more than the last. When her eyes drifted shut, he moved to her forehead and skimmed his lips lightly down her face, pausing warmly on her eyelids and the tip of her pert nose. The corners of her mouth beckoned for his attention, and he gave in to the urge to dip his tongue along the edges, enticing her into a tremulous response. He leaned back then, arms braced on the wall on either side of her. Her breathing had grown shallow and rapid, her cheeks flushed with desire.

"Meggie?" Steven whispered against her mouth.

"Hmm?"

"May I kiss you now?"

She made a throaty sound and opened her eyes. They looked drowsy with passion, a little unfocused. Her head dipped almost imperceptibly in answer to his question. But before he had a chance to lower his head, she framed his face with determined hands and did it for him, offering her sweetness for him to savor.

Steven groaned when he covered her mouth almost violently and took what he'd been dreaming of for days, the hot, arousing taste of heaven that was Meg. Her hands grasped fistfuls of hair, the impatient tug bringing his entire body into intimate contact with hers. Pressing her back urgently to the wall, he forgot his plan to exercise self-discipline and kissed her hungrily, turning his head this way and the other to gain better access. He burrowed beneath her tank top to the heated skin of her midriff and rubbed her navel with the pad of his thumb, provoking a small gasp. She wrapped her arms around his neck tightly and sought to capture his delving tongue, stroking it with her own in a rhythm as old as time.

Finally, they came up for air, but only long enough to adjust their position so he could push up her top and fondle the taut globes of her breasts. Meg's head fell back, and he kept his eyes locked with hers as he squeezed and plucked erotically at her nipples, her sensuous moans spurring him on to place burning kisses where his hands had roamed just a second before. The dig of her nails in his scalp barely registered and he pulled moistly on her breast, trying to take as much of her inside as possible.

"Steven," she whispered raggedly, drawing him up for another kiss, "could we move this to my room? It's a little hard getting you undressed."

Unaware that she had divested him of his tie and unbuttoned his shirt, he blinked dazedly. "I'm sorry. I didn't mean to get carried away." *My God, she's beautiful, and I'm not one bit sorry. Except for one thing.* "I wasn't prepared for this."

"I don't know if I'm ready, either, but I want you." Meg's blunt statement went straight to his already aching manhood.

"I want you, too, but I meant . . . ah . . . condoms. I don't have any." He rested his forehead on hers and tried not to notice her bare chest brushing his.

"I do."

"Really?" Grinning his intoxication, he kissed her again. "Then maybe we could try one out."

Meg smiled seductively and hauled her tank top over her head.

"You are the loveliest woman I have ever laid eyes on," he rasped, tracing the line of one smooth shoulder. If he made it to the bedroom, he'd be a lucky man.

"Then make love to me." She pushed his shirt off and let it drop to the floor. Taking his hand, she placed it over her heart and whispered, "Show me, Steven."

Unwilling to give either of them the chance to have second thoughts, he scooped her up and took her to the big brass bed he'd seen so many times in his imaginings. Carefully setting her down in the middle of the mattress, he simply looked at her for a minute, taking in the flaming hair spread across the pillow, the fullness of her proud breasts, the direct blue gaze as she held out her arms and lured him down.

Meg couldn't get enough of him, couldn't stop touching his hard body wherever she could reach. His skin was afire, the sleekness of him burning under the ardent glide of her hands on his back. He promised pleasure beyond description with murmured phrases, the raw undertones sharpening her awareness of how stimulated he was. Every kiss and stroke set her senses ablaze and left her teetering on the edge of oblivion. She banished all thoughts from her mind but those of Steven and what he was doing to her, uncaring if she awoke to discover it was just a wonderfully vivid fantasy.

It had taken them mere moments to strip what remained of their clothes and come together beneath the blankets, both anxious to feel the explosive passion that consumed them whenever they made contact.

Meg's blistering gaze had devoured his nakedness in the instant before he slid in beside her, pausing wantonly on the thickened length of him. He was breathtakingly exquisite, and she told him so, even while she wondered desperately if she could satisfy this powerful, sexy man with her lack of experience. The notion evaporated like fog in bright sunlight when he pulled her to him, the heat in his stare all the encouragement she needed to meet him halfway.

Now, as she roved her covetous hands down his back once more, he rose onto his elbows to rub his erection on her belly. Meg was awed by the fierce look in his eyes, the flush on his hard cheekbones. She grasped his behind and lifted her legs, locking knees around lean hips and arching the center of her desire against him recklessly. He stilled her movements then, the grim set of his mouth telling her he would be teased no more.

"Careful, darling," Steven rasped, closing his eyes tightly. "I want this to last."

He eased away, and Meg rolled to one side to rummage for the box she'd stashed in the nightstand. Shakily extracting a foil package, she handed it to him and watched, fascinated, when he readied himself.

Flinging the empty packet over the side of the bed, he enquired naughtily, "Enjoying yourself?"

"Immensely. Can I touch you?" Meg's smile widened further when he placed her trembling hand upon him and folded both of his comfortably under his head.

"Be nice now. I'm delicate."

She laughed at that. "This doesn't feel delicate," she observed and cupped him, massaging slowly. "How's that?"

Steven only groaned and tilted his pelvis to accommodate her probing hand. His chest and neck glistened with sweat, and as she watched, he swallowed with difficulty.

"Am I hurting you?" she asked softly, her attention centered on the rigid line of him while she moved back and forth with lazy strokes.

"Damn right, but that's not a complaint. Here, like this."

Pushing her down, he kissed her deeply. He slipped a hand between her thighs, and she jerked convulsively, the expert touch causing more of a reaction than she anticipated.

"Easy, love. It only gets better."

"Now," she pleaded breathlessly. "Do it now."

Steven laughed a little wickedly but obliged her by settling himself between her legs and seeking entry. "Okay?"

Meg nodded, her muscles clenching involuntarily for the pain she knew would come. "Please."

He levered his body down and forward, pausing when she couldn't hide a wince. The discomfort ebbed, and she urged him closer, but he stopped, the too-tight sheath all the proof he needed that this was her first time.

"Don't you dare stop now," she warned.

"You should have told me, Meggie." His jaw clenched, but he didn't move away.

"Does it matter?"

"God, yes!" He heaved himself off her and lay on his back, one arm thrown across his eyes. "Of course, it matters. You should be wined and dined and cherished for hours before—"

"I was feeling quite cherished, actually, before you shrank from me in disgust." Suddenly self-conscious of her nudity, Meg yanked the blankets up to her chin.

"That wasn't what happened. Let me explain."

"Forget it."

"No." Steven pulled her back into his embrace and refused to let go, no matter how much she wriggled and cursed him. After a lively tussle, she gave up. "Ready to listen?"

She huffed, exasperated. "It's no big deal, really. So, you're one of those men who doesn't want the responsibility of taking a girl's virginity. I understand. The prospect of having my undying gratitude is too much to bear."

"You're full of it. Just for your information, I'd be thrilled to have your undying—"

"I absolve you of any and all accountability for relieving me of my maidenhead. Okay? Can we do it now?" she muttered into the curve of his neck, face aflame.

Steven laughed. Not the uncomfortable laugh of a man in hot water, but the uproarious, bellyaching laugh of a man who was plainly amused. When he eventually calmed down, he said, "Your use of archaic terms is unique. I don't recall ever hearing anyone say *maidenhead* out loud."

Meg punched him.

"I only meant—about your virginity—that if I'd known, I would have gone more slowly, took my time and made sure it wasn't so uncomfortable for you. I don't want to rush through like a randy teenager. Jeez, Meg," he whispered, hugging her close, "I don't want to hurt you."

She sighed, partly glad he was so thoughtful, partly peeved he'd been in control enough to stop.

"We could start from the beginning," he slyly suggested.

Lifting a shoulder as if she cared not one way or the other, she replied, "No, thanks. I have to put Baz to bed anyway." She grabbed her robe from the foot of the bed and squirmed into it. "It's just as well you wanted me to meet some of your family first. I'll feel better knowing I'm pure."

"Baz? Pure?" he hollered after her. "You're a mean, mean woman, Meg Layton."

The mean woman only smiled and fetched Baz some

berries.

CHAPTER SIX

"I don't think this is such a good idea, Steven." The dread in her voice was just one more hint in a long line of them that Meg was agitated. She was not looking forward to this evening at all and she didn't mind letting him know it. So far, she'd changed her clothes and hairdo three times, checked her slim, gold watch six times, and claimed Baz didn't look well twice.

Steven was feeling a bit edgy himself. "It's only for a couple of hours. You're going to love them. Stop pacing like that." He went to the bathroom and knotted his tie quickly, wanting to get her out to the car before she changed her mind. It would be his luck if she did, considering the rotten day he'd had. Meg Layton was causing him a lot of sleepless nights. The upside of it was she seemed to be having just as much trouble.

After refusing to leave her bed last night, he'd been tortured by the scent of her on the pillows while she supposedly *slept* on his. The minor spat over her virginity — if you could call it a spat — had carried over to the breakfast table. Meg had ignored him for the most part, speaking only in monosyllables when she felt like it. He'd finally slammed out of the apartment and to work, a chip the size of a two-by-four on his shoulder.

It didn't pay to be noble these days, he brooded now to his reflection. So, as soon as they got home tonight, he was going to give the redheaded minx what she'd asked for. If he didn't rip that clingy white piece of silk from her body before they even made it to dinner, that was. The last outfit change had robbed his breath, the revealing dress floating about her long legs and snuggling her perfect chest. She'd pinned up her hair in a mass of riotous ringlets, exposing the elegant line of her neck for all to see. He was convinced she'd done it on purpose just to aggravate him.

"Did I leave my wrap in here?" She appeared in the doorway, all creamy shoulders and glossy lips. Her eyes were darkened dramatically with a touch of makeup, her skin scented with a dab of elusive perfume.

"Pardon?" Steven tore his gaze from her with enormous effort. He was in dire need of more oxygen.

"My wrap. Never mind, I think I put it in the living room." She turned to go, then paused and said shyly, "You look good."

The compliment served as a balm to his ego. He was still concerned about how she'd react to his family, and that was irritating. Surely she'd see what a loving and devoted bunch they were. Wouldn't she? Or would she suffer through the evening determined not to like them despite how well they treated her? That was a dampening notion.

"Ready?" he asked when he joined her in the kitchen.

Meg fingered a curl and drew a deep breath. "Are you sure you want to do this? I mean, they'll probably hate me on sight. I'm no good at faking this family stuff, Steven. I honestly don't have a clue how to act."

"Sweetheart, you don't have to fake a thing." Taking hold of her arms tenderly, he dropped a kiss on her mouth. "You're my date. Just be yourself. It'll just be Viv and Jonas and maybe his mother, Eleuthera. Relax."

"I can't."

"Try. For me," he added solemnly. "I did manage to scare off your parents for a few days. The very least you can do is enjoy yourself."

Alice and Harry hadn't called Meg or come by to visit, and he couldn't tell if she was hurt or relieved. He was really ticked that they seemed to pop in and out of her life on impulse. It was no wonder she had difficulty developing relationships based on more than friendship.

"I don't feel right," she muttered, bringing him back to the present. "They expect us to be a couple, and we're not."

"We are."

"No, we're—"

Steven kissed her. Long and deep and intensely. When he eventually released her, her lip gloss was gone, and her eyes glittered excitedly. "We are," he repeated firmly, "and we're going to be lovers before this night is over."

Meg opened her mouth and closed it again.

"No objection?" He was amazed.

"Look what you've done to my lipstick!"

The Mackenzie estate was elegant and warm, the exact opposite of her grandfather's. Meg marveled at the difference privately while she examined the newly redecorated mansion. Her mother's father, who had left Meg a chunk of money that was a bone of contention between her parents, had loved to flaunt his wealth, a trait that had rubbed off on Alice. His house had always looked expensive and frighteningly austere. Not like this one.

"This is lovely," she whispered to Steven, the gorgeous flowers spilling over pots in the entryway catching her artistic eye.

"It hasn't been this cheery for long. Eleuthera decided recently to step out of the past and brighten the place up. Having Viv to help was good for her."

They were shown to a large solarium where a couple stood, their arms entwined as they took in the stars above.

One bright, blonde head rested against the broad shoulder of a very big man, the woman leaning trustingly into his embrace. The scene looked too intimate to be interrupted, but as she was on the verge of suggesting to Steven that they wait, Viv Mackenzie turned and smiled. The redhead beside her followed suit, and introductions were made.

"So, you're the saint who's tolerating my cousin while the plumber does his job." Viv shook hands and ran one over her swelling stomach. "Don't let him in the kitchen."

"He's already warned me." Meg laughed, liking the attractive woman instantly. Then she took in the bear of a man whose brown eyes twinkled. "Jonas, I presume. It's nice to meet you."

"You presume correctly. It's a pleasure to have you in our home." He grinned and told Steven, "I don't see any warts."

Meg frowned in confusion, and he replied, "They disappeared when she got a look at me." Slipping an arm around her waist, he explained, "Jonas only stopped pestering me about my new neighbour when I swore you were duck ugly. Forgive the lie. He's just impossibly nosy."

Viv clucked dryly. "It runs around that company if you ask me."

"I did notice that Steven is a bit inquisitive. Is he always that way?" Meg prodded smilingly.

"Yes."

"Is this a Steven Roast?" he demanded of his partner.

Jonas shrugged. "If the shoe fits . . ."

"Don't poison her mind. I've had a struggle getting her this far."

Viv linked her arm with Meg's and pulled her aside, leaving the men to have a good-natured squabble. "I hope you aren't overwhelmed with us." She grimaced apologetically. "We tried to keep the dinner quiet, but the twins figured it out and called in The Parents."

Meg's eyes widened when she realized what Viv was telling her. At the same time, Steven had overheard, and his shoulders lifted as if to say, *I didn't know a thing about it.*

"Ma Janey and Pop will be arriving with the twins," her hostess went on, oblivious to her rising panic. "I believe they're staying for a week."

"Can I get you a drink, Meg?" Steven slid a hand into hers, and she gripped it tightly. "A double, perhaps?" he mumbled in an undertone.

"Some wine would be nice."

He gave her another squeeze and winked secretly. "I'll be right back."

Meg tried to smile at Viv, who had observed the exchange closely. "This is a bit new for me — meeting someone's family. I didn't think it would be so soon."

The pregnant woman nodded as if in approval of her having confessed to not meeting a man's parents before. "Don't be nervous. They're wonderful. We call them The Parents because they seem to adopt everybody in sight."

"Um, how far along are you?" Meg timidly asked, aching to change the subject.

"Nearly six months." Viv beamed radiantly. "I can't wait. Do you like kids?"

"Love them. I have two friends who let me spoil theirs rotten."

"You're planning to have some of your own then?"

She was saved from having to answer that question as Steven returned with her wine. Accepting it gratefully, she hid behind the distraction a bit guiltily. She didn't want to deal with the dicey issue of children, no matter how well-meaning the enquiry.

The foursome chatted amiably for a while longer before they were joined by Eleuthera Mackenzie, who swept into the solarium on the arm of a very distinguished-looking gentleman. She smiled benignly at Meg and introduced her escort, Dr. Fred Reynolds, who was obviously smitten with the dark-haired woman.

"It's a pleasure, my dear," the graying doctor said, taking Meg's hand. His faded blue eyes still held an irreverent gleam, his grin infectious, and he bowed in a courtly manner. "You aren't, by chance, related to the late Niles Layton?" he asked, a note of sobriety entering his voice. He covered it well, but she caught it nonetheless.

"Niles was my grandfather," she responded evenly. Noting the confusion clouding his features—for Niles had no sons, just a daughter—she added dryly, "My parents coincidentally had the same surname—very distant cousins. Mother would have kept her maiden name and given it to me at Niles' decree anyhow." She saw then that Eleuthera's ears had perked up at the mention of the domineering real estate mogul. The others had moved away, and she suddenly wished for Steven's comforting presence. Niles had not been a particularly popular man, some of his dealings rumoured to be downright despicable, so it wouldn't really surprise her if Fred and Eleuthera remembered him with distaste. That was how she'd felt about him for most of her life and the main reason she'd adamantly rejected the money he'd left her. After having discovered that he'd shafted many an innocent in his business ventures, she considered that the trust fund was made off the backs of vulnerable people and, therefore, contaminated with greed.

"Then you *are* Alice's daughter," Fred murmured thoughtfully, this time drawing the attention of his date with his odd tone.

Meg only nodded, strangely uneasy now with the way the older man was looking at her. His gaze roamed her face deliberately, as if seeking a resemblance to her mother.

"I don't look much like her," she supplied, getting a little annoyed. "Did you know Alice?"

"Yes." Fred's grin faltered momentarily. "I'm glad you kept your hair that color. She always detested hers, said blonde was more sophisticated."

That was precisely what Meg's mother had told her all of her young life, insisting that she bleach out the red tresses. She had refused stubbornly.

Just how well had Dr. Reynolds known Alice? And why did he seem so familiar to Meg, who was certain she'd never met him before tonight?

Steven put an arm around her, dislodging her train of thought. She smiled with relief and took a fortifying sip of wine.

A flurry of activity out in the hall announced the arrival of the rest of the dinner guests. Eleuthera excused herself and tugged her beau along to greet them. Minutes later, Meg was introduced to Cass and Caro, two gorgeous brunettes with eyes that matched their brother's, and a couple in their late fifties. Ma Janey, as Meg was instructed warmly to call her, hugged her as if she were already kin. Jon Kincaid watched in amusement and raised bushy gray eyebrows while his wife prattled animatedly over her son's *girlfriend*. She flicked a glance at Steven, a little irked that he'd presumed to use the term to his mother. Unrepentant, he tightened his hold on her waist and caught up on news with the clan.

Meg discovered many things that evening. Mostly, she realized she didn't fit in. Not that anyone tried to shut her out of a conversation. In fact, they appeared to relish the opportunity to extol the virtues and expound on the childhood escapades of her roommate. Steven suffered the endless comic stories patiently, once or twice blushing over an incident that embarrassed him.

The whole lot of them jousted and sparred with the ease

born of experience and acceptance. This was uncommon for Meg, who'd been told as a child that dinnertime was for eating, not talk, and it was rude to tease anyone playfully about anything at any time. So, feeling a bit at a loss, she sat quietly and enjoyed the banter going on around her.

The twins were a revelation, as Meg had never witnessed two people who so closely resembled each other in appearance yet not one whit in personality. Caro talked a mile a minute, often engaging in bouts of jesting disagreement while Cass spoke rarely except with a quirk of the eyebrow or lip, a trait the others deemed adorable if slightly maddening.

Off and on throughout the evening, Meg felt the concentrated scrutiny of Fred Reynolds, who had also refrained from participating in much conversation. Curiously, whenever she turned her head to catch his stare, he smiled almost imperceptibly. The enigmatic expression he wore was unnerving, and by the time dessert was served she was itching to leave.

Steven, sensing her discomfort, drew her aside when everyone returned to the solarium for an after-dinner drink. "I can see you aren't having a good time, Meg. Why don't I make some excuse and we'll go home now?" His jaw was tense, his shoulders rigid.

It dawned on her then that he thought she wanted to leave because of his family.

"I'd rather stay, actually," she bravely contradicted. "I haven't heard yet how you managed to get out of the neighbour's apple tree without getting caught."

He relaxed visibly and sighed. "I *did* get caught. If I hadn't, I would be spared tons of humiliation."

She chuckled wickedly. "Serves you right."

"Mmm. They like you, you know."

"How can you tell?"

"Ma never shares recipes with people she doesn't like."

"I figured she just didn't want you to starve while you're living with me." She grinned, though, because she found that she wanted his family's approval. "I like them, too."

"So why are you so eager to get home?" Steven's eyes narrowed. "You want to get me in bed. I knew it! You're dying to put your salacious hands on my body."

"I told you, I want to stay."

"Uh-huh. Your mouth says that, but your eyes say *Take me home.*"

Meg poked him in the ribs. "You're projecting. It's *you* who's impatient to get beneath the sheets. I can wait."

He placed a hand over his heart. "You are a cold woman."

"Is that an improvement on mean?" she sweetly enquired, referring to the label he'd put on her last night.

"It's just as bad." He dropped the woeful look and turned serious. "Are you sure you're not uncomfortable?"

Meg decided to explain about her grandfather and Fred and Eleuthera's reaction to her. "It was a bit unusual, but it passed. Jonas' mother isn't holding my relatives against me. I'm not so certain about Fred. He's been giving me strange looks all evening."

"Maybe he was one of the people Niles bilked out of their money."

"It's possible, but I think it's even more personal than that. He knew Alice." Meg chewed on her lower lip, worrying the tender skin until Steven stopped her with a kiss.

"Leave that for me. I want to use them both—top and bottom."

They joined the others but declined another drink, Meg having reached her limit and Steven in possession of the car keys. She offered to drive back if he wished to imbibe one more, but he whispered in her ear that he intended to remain very sober for when they got home.

"I don't think we ought to sleep together tonight," she hissed back. "Everyone will think we hurried off to jump in the sack."

He laughed. "They'll assume that anyway. And I'm all for the hurrying part."

"You weren't last night."

"I mean, I want to get there as soon as possible, but the rest will take all night."

Meg blushed furiously. "Oh."

"What are you two whispering about?" Viv prompted lowly. "Is he trying to get you to leave, Meg? Shame on you!" she chided Steven. "I thought you had better sense than to try seducing her with The Parents in the room."

"I can't wear her down," he admitted. "She's pure."

Viv cast a dubious glance Meg's way. "You saved yourself for this?"

"I'm considering it," she acknowledged, astonished that it was true.

The party broke up shortly after that, and Meg was settling her wrap around her shoulders with Steven's help when Fred Reynolds approached. She kept a firm grip on her purse and her date's arm as he stopped in front of them and asked, "How are Alice and Harry these days? Do they visit often?"

"They're doing fine . . . and in town now." She was reluctant to add anything further. As kind and gentle as the doctor seemed, he was still a stranger and not entitled to know about her strained relationship with her parents. "I'll give them your regards."

Fred smiled somewhat grimly and bade them goodnight. "I hope to see you again," he told Meg cryptically.

Steven regarded the older man surreptitiously when they

left, noting that he had bestowed an inordinate amount of attention on Meg. It wasn't blatant, at least not to anyone except him and Eleuthera, but Fred appeared to focus singularly on his new acquaintance. He shoved the notion aside, putting the man's interest down to simple appreciation of beauty. Who wouldn't be enthralled with Meg Layton?

The prospect of what would happen when they got to the apartment meant his foot was heavier than usual on the accelerator. His passenger either shared the same thoughts or was too absorbed in others to object to the speed with which they crossed town. The car's wheels squealed as he turned it into the driveway, and she laughed breathlessly when it came to a halt.

Meg alighted before he had a chance to round the car, her long legs taking her up the steps, and he followed closely.

Once inside, he locked the door and reached for her.

"Shouldn't we check on Baz?" Meg wrestled impatiently with his tie. His jacket fell to the floor, and she started on buttons. "He's probably hungry."

As if on cue, the neglected bird shrieked from his cage in Meg's room, demanding that someone pamper him directly.

"I'll get him," Steven volunteered, averse to having the night interrupted periodically. Shirtless, he strode to the back room and retrieved the cage. He made a pit stop in the kitchen for some nuts and dried fruit and continued past the puzzled redhead and on to his apartment. There, he freed the cockatoo and filled a small bowl with water to place on the floor. Newspaper completed the list of requirements for an overnight stay.

"I'll leave a light on," he promised Baz when he trotted out from confinement. "You have lots of space here. Just do me a favor and don't squawk, buddy, or it'll be back to Peabody's Pets for you. Got it?"

Baz selected a dried fig from the tray and dipped his

head.

"Good. One of us will be back in the morning to get you. If the plumber shows before then, don't run him off. He's already days late getting started." He headed for the door, then paused to remind the bird, "You can't poop on my furniture either."

Meg had pulled the pins from her hair and was in the process of undressing in her room. "What did you do with him?"

"Who?" The vision of her in nothing more than a slip and high heels was muddying up his brain. A certain part of his anatomy responded to the ocular treat.

"Bazil."

"He's safe. Next door. Stop that."

"What?" she asked in confusion.

"I want to undress you."

"It's nearly done now."

"Yes," he exhaled longingly, "you've deprived me. Now, leave that scrap for me to deal with."

Meg came toward him then and unfastened his belt. "You're too slow, Kincaid."

"I'm waiting for my heart to regulate itself." He grasped her hands and held them behind her back, arching her into him. "Feel that? That's what the thought of finally being with you does to me."

"Oh my."

Steven cupped her bottom and ground his erection against her. Her head fell back, and she whimpered incoherently, moving her hips in time with his. Over and over, she pushed at him, and he reveled in the tantalizing rhythm until he couldn't stand any more without disgracing himself.

"You're so beautiful," he said raggedly, grabbing the hem of her slip and tugging it off to expose her naked breasts. They filled his hands perfectly, the tips beading under his rapt encouragement.

Meg lifted her mouth for his kiss, and he obliged fiercely, aching to taste her softness. He drove his tongue inside and groaned, feeling her nails score his back. A sharp pleasure-pain raced through his blood and swelled his manhood to excruciating hardness.

The need to be one with her overtook him, and without another sane thought, he fell onto the bed, his legs tangling with hers even while he struggled to remove his pants. He tore the last wisp of fabric from her, and she cried out urgently, shoving him down on the pillows and mounting him.

"Easy, love," he rasped, forestalling his entry with commendable restraint. Rolling her beneath him, he whispered, "It will hurt less this way."

"If you say so." She smiled beautifully. "But next time, I get to be on top."

"Deal." Steven shifted and probed her moistness, the sleek texture of her desire nearly sending him over the edge. Carefully, he eased inside her, withdrawing slightly, and she gasped.

"No, don't stop." Her eyes were the bluest he'd ever seen them, and misty with passion. "Deeper, Steven."

When he felt the thin barrier give, he buried his cock to the hilt and stayed motionless until she lifted her gaze to his once more and tightened her muscles hesitantly.

"Okay?" he murmured tenderly, extracting another kiss. Then he settled his weight more intimately upon her.

"Okay." She smiled and laughed, the husky sound going right to his very soul and warming him from the inside out.

In that instant, Steven knew he couldn't live without her, would fight any demons, real or imagined, to keep her by his side. The words he yearned to utter were on the tip of his tongue and would have tripped off if not for the nagging voice in his head that warned they might scare her. Instead, he moved gradually, intent on drawing out her pleasure and holding back for his own.

"Damn." Abruptly, he realized he wasn't wearing protection. "Sorry, Meggie," he apologized and eased from her.

She looked mystified for a moment, but then her frown disappeared. "I can't believe that slipped my mind."

"No harm done." He joined her again after a moment and coaxed her legs around him. "Will you tell me if I'm hurting you?"

Meg nodded, locking her arms behind his back. "I think the pain has passed. Mmm. Oh, yes, it's definitely gone."

Their bodies glided over one another sensuously, rocking in an amorous tempo as they kissed and caressed more heatedly with each stroke. Soon, the steady pace wasn't enough for either of them, and the pattern grew frantic, the bed squeaking.

She bit his shoulder erotically, spurring him on to thrust faster and harder and deeper. She called his name when the spasms came, her muscles clenched, and she gave in to her climax. He slammed into her wildly, the bed frame hitting the wall, sending her into the throes of a second orgasm. His own release impacted with mind-shattering force, and he collapsed on top of her, spent.

The soothing touch of Meg's hands roused him a short time later, the affectionate massage on his back stirring him anew.

"Wow," she breathed against his cheek.

"You can say that again," Steven mumbled into her neck. "Are you all right?"

"Mmm-hmm. Wonderful."

Propping himself carefully on his elbows, he searched her face. Her eyes were closed peacefully, her skin still flushed. She slid her hands down to his behind and pressed his burgeoning arousal into her.

"How can you be ready again so soon?" she queried drowsily. "I didn't know it was possible."

"Neither did I. Want to stop?"

In answer, she undulated her hips slowly.

Steven chuckled and let her take him.

Hours later, he awoke to find Meg gone. Sounds from the kitchen had him reaching blindly beside the bed for his pants. When he ambled to the other room yawning and scratching his chin, she turned from the refrigerator with an armful of food.

"I got hungry," she said, dumping her load on the table. "Want a sandwich?"

"Sure." There was something infinitely sexy about the way his shirt draped over her nude body. The sleeves flopped past her hands, cuffs unbuttoned, and it drifted to mid-thigh, skimming her firm flesh. "Just put—"

"—everything on it. I know."

"You're getting used to me."

Meg sliced the heaping creation in two and set about making her own smaller one. "Are all men bottomless pits?"

"Only the lucky ones." He sat and bit off a chunk of sandwich, ignoring her when she clucked and shook her head. "I'm a big boy. I take big bites."

"I noticed." Her look said she was alluding to things other than food.

Steven swallowed with difficulty, and she scooted her chair in, revealing the swell of her breasts as his too-large shirt gaped and resettled. He dropped his snack and forgot about it.

"You'd better finish that. I distinctly remember you saying a certain activity would take all night. You'll need your strength." She delicately licked a smear of mayo from her lips.

"I'd rather watch you eat. Besides, I can't drag you back to bed and ravish you all night."

"Why not?"

"Well . . . because . . ."

Meg's eyebrow lifted.

"You got that from Cass," he accused.

"She's better at it. Why can't we do it again?"

He ate the rest of the crust and tried to recall what his reasoning had been. "Mmph."

"What?"

"It's your first time. I should have been more considerate."

She grinned cheekily. "You were incredible."

"But I don't want you to hurt in the morning."

Squirming a little, she remarked, "I am a bit tender. I expected worse."

"Then you see why we can't—what are you doing?" he demanded when she came around and straddled his lap. "Meg, I don't have a—"

"I do." She fished a foil packet from his shirt pocket. "I thought you might follow me."

So rapidly did she unzip his trousers and free him that he wondered how she got to be that efficient.

"I was imagining what it would be like to do this here," she replied when he mentioned it. "Only I figured you'd be more help."

"I was being careful of you."

As she sank down on him and cuddled closer, her lids fluttered shut, and she moaned softly. "You feel so good."

"Tell me," Steven urged.

And she did.

In the morning, Baz let them know he was heartily sick of being overlooked. The incessant screeching coming from next door was accompanied by a series of knocks and shuffles. What he'd managed to find to demonstrate his displeasure with became apparent when Steven trailed him into the kitchen.

Every canister had been overturned and nudged off the counter and now rested on the floor, the contents spilled on the tiles. Coffee, sugar, flour—which Steven kept but had no use for—littered the room from one corner to the other.

The cockatoo's black beak was dusted with white powder. He glared at Steven and stomped through his mess arrogantly, clearly satisfied that his point was made. Then, apparently not happy with the idea that his ire was contained in one room, strutted to the living area and vengefully hopped from the couch to the armchair and back, leaving a ghostly set of tracks in his wake.

"I'm sorry." Steven crouched and wiped the flour from Bazil's nose, hoping fervently that exotic birds didn't sneeze. "We slept in. It was a long night."

"Are you talking to the bird?" Meg appeared in the doorway, sunlight framing her fiery hair.

"I always talk to Baz."

"Really?" she prompted warily.

He lifted their charge to one shoulder and stood. "You've heard me do that before."

"Yes, but I don't know if I should worry that you feel accountable to him for your actions."

"He's made a mess in my kitchen. I'll have to clean up. Will you take him over?"

Meg sighed. "Does this mean we have to abstain from—" she glanced at the bird as if concerned for his sensitive ears "—sex?"

Baz squawked and bobbed his head up and down.

"He'll adjust. I only wanted him here so as not to be a distraction on our first night together."

"Oh good. I refuse to have my needs put off according to

108

Bazil's whims. I don't care how cute he is."

Baz preened at the compliment.

"You need me?" Steven edged closer and kissed her, unbalancing the bird in the process. "I believe I'm touched."

"You're a fantastic lover. Don't let it go to your head." She tossed her hair back and tapped her shoulder, the signal Baz understood as *come here – please*. He did.

"I won't be long," Steven called after the retreating duo.

The woman waved a hand behind her bright head. The bird scowled.

CHAPTER SEVEN

The next two days went better than Meg could ever have dreamed. She had settled into somewhat of a routine with her lover and was surprised to find she was not at all uncomfortable with the shared intimacy. The sight of his razor and cologne amongst her toiletries was not as alien as when he'd moved in. She liked bumping into him as he got ready for work and liked making him late even more.

The plumber had commenced his battle with the pipes in Steven's apartment and had disturbed the couple early two mornings in a row. Never one to pass up an opportunity, Steven coaxed Meg into some very creative lovemaking instead of going back to sleep.

Baz had accepted the relationship gracefully for the time being and declined to follow the urge to remind the humans of his presence. As long as he was fed and watered, he was moderately content. Although he did preen now and then to see if they'd notice there was another living organism on the planet besides each other. They didn't.

Meg knew The Parents called several times to chat with their son and had been put off from issuing an invitation to Cass and Caro's house for dinner. Steven claimed that he and Meg both had worked piled up and promised to get together before they returned to Bay de Chance. He told her that was only half true, that the idea of splitting his attention between Meg and anything or anyone at the moment did not appeal. That was selfish, he'd admitted, but he figured he was due.

Meg was a trifle uneasy about a message left on her machine one day from Arthur Muldoon, her grandfather's lawyer. A cryptic warning that her parents might be contacting her soon was a bit late in coming, and she hadn't been able to catch the man in his office afterward. So, when Alice called to invite her to the hotel for drinks on Friday, she quizzed her about the message. Alice was vague, the unnaturally high pitch of her laughter when she brushed off the subject of Old Arthur making Meg think she'd better be mindful of her parents' motives.

Managing to persuade her to forget her screwy relatives — for he said he was convinced they were definitely missing a few links in their gate chain — Steven took Meg to a play and a late dinner at an exclusive restaurant. There, he'd had a private room complete with violin player. They danced and whispered to each other before he'd professed he'd become too bothered to stay for dessert and whisked her home and to bed.

As he lay stroking her hair and waiting for his breathing to return to normal, he remarked, "That painting is good."

"Hmm?" Meg snuggled closer and kissed his collarbone.

"The unicorn thingy on the ceiling."

"Is this the first time you noticed it?"

"No, I spent hours looking at it that night you so cruelly left me here alone. Don't laugh. I was lonely. The unicorn made a great sounding board." He waited for her to stop giggling. "Baz isn't very sympathetic. He talks back."

"What did you say to my sensitive unicorn?"

"I said, Chester —"

Meg rolled on her back and howled.

He ignored her comic response and continued, "Chester, your mistress is a hardened individual. I need some serious affection."

"And did he answer you?"

"No. Stop laughing! I told you, he doesn't talk back. He's an understanding soul."

"He's paint."

Steven pounced on her and growled, "Don't mock my friend. He was all I had when you left me here by myself."

"I'm sorry," she said solemnly. "I won't leave you in such a state again."

"That's nice to hear. Hmm."

"What?"

"I believe I'm entering that realm right now." He grinned in the dark.

"Oh, so you are." Meg wiggled beneath him and sighed. "You are a beautiful man."

No more was spoken until morning.

"You're keeping her locked away from the family," Caro huffed over the phone. "The poor woman needs interaction, Steven, not mauling to death."

Steven logged off his computer for the day and leaned back to view the St. John's harbor. "Don't be silly, sis. I'm only mauling her into exhaustion."

A strangled noise echoed as a reply.

"Caro, this is new for Meg. I don't want her run off by my well-meaning family members."

His sister sighed. "Is she coming along?"

"Uh-huh. Now, butt out," he ordered grimly and hung up.

The phone call was not the only thing bugging him. Meg was still referring to their relationship in the temporary sense. Twice she had made comments alluding to his return to the apartment next door. She'd said that he might want to see about getting Baz a mate when he went *home* and maybe he ought to ask Rupert to get *his* doorway fixed. She talked as if he would be moving out any day now.

Steven smiled. He was going nowhere for another three weeks. The plumber had informed him just that morning that he was waiting on some special pipe joints, grumbling that someone should have replaced the ancient stuff decades ago.

No, his darling was stuck with him a while longer. Long enough for him to make her see he was serious about a commitment. He was more certain of their compatibility now that they'd spent several days together.

Meg's personality only endeared her to him. Her touchy temper when he needled her — even though she claimed not to be moody in the least — her sassy mouth and cheeky sense of humour, the nervous habit of nibbling her lower lip, the way she purred while he rubbed her neck and moaned softly when he kissed her.

What amazed him the most was that she had not one inkling of how seductive and alluring she was. There was no coyness about her, no affected come-hither look to draw him to her. Sometimes she seemed stumped if he told her how he wanted her, her eyes going blank before she registered that he was sincere and then turning languid, leaning into his embrace and going with him to the bedroom. She held nothing back there, giving herself to him openly and freely.

However, she remained firm in her description of their relationship as an affair, more so after the few phone calls from her mother. Her lips compressed, and she cradled the receiver, her eyes narrowed, every part of her tense as she silently stalked back to her drawing board and immersed herself in work. It was those times that he felt shut out and he sensed she did it deliberately.

"The twins are having a barbecue on Saturday," he mentioned that night at the table. He avoided looking at her directly but didn't miss the way her body went rigid. He went on, "They want us to come."

Meg was quiet for an unusually long time before she asked, "Will your parents be there?"

He lifted his gaze to watch her push food around her plate. "Yes, they're still in town. Half the neighborhood will probably be there by the time Ma's through." He paused. "You're chewing your lip again."

"Olaf is coming on Saturday for another sitting."

"No, he isn't. He called yesterday, remember? He's taking Fannie camping this weekend."

"Oh, right. Then I guess it's okay."

"Don't sound so excited, Meg. I wouldn't want you to put yourself out or anything," he said stiffly, shoving his chair back. He brought his dishes to the sink and rinsed them with choppy movements. No sound came from behind him, and a tinge of remorse twisted inside him for snapping at her. Hadn't he known this would be a struggle? She had let him know from the first that she didn't want to get tangled up with his relatives while they had their *affair*.

"I'm sorry." Her gentle voice wobbled slightly. "I like your family, it's just—"

Steven turned, drew her to her feet, and held her close. "I know. I'm sorry, too. I don't want you to do anything you're not comfortable with." He kissed the top of her bright head and rocked back and forth, the motion calming them both while they stood that way for a long time.

"Will your sisters mind if I bring something?" Meg mumbled into his shirt.

He chuckled, the tension leaving him. "Are you kidding? The more food, the happier us men will be. We can go early and help them set up. That is, if you're sure?"

She nodded. "This is hard for me, Steven."

"I know. But I'll be with you all the way, every time. Got it?" If she didn't, she would sooner or later. He'd make damn sure she knew he intended to stick around and stick close.

The hotel restaurant was humming with the clink of silverware and subdued conversation as Meg waited for Alice to join her. The offer of drinks had expanded to include dinner for just the two of them once Harry had been given the chance to busy himself elsewhere. That was how her father traditionally behaved when faced with spending time at the same table as Meg for any more than the twenty minutes it took to consume a meal. At least this way she only had to contend with her mother.

Another message had been on her machine from Arthur Muldoon, and Meg could only guess he wanted to discuss her trust fund. Since she couldn't care less if the whole lot of it burned, she was in no hurry to speak with him. She had tried to reach him, however, as a common courtesy to the aging gent. Arthur had always been sweet to her, even under the scowling disapproval of her grandfather. Unfortunately, he was a touch scattered these days and neglected to leave his home or cell number, so she'd missed him again.

Glancing at her watch, she saw that Alice was late. She wondered how long she'd be left cooling her heels this time. Her mother didn't consider that making somebody wait was thoughtless, just that it showed who had the upper hand in every meeting—and she did like to have control of the situation. Even with her only child. *Especially* with her.

Finally, the older woman appeared, smiling brightly with just the right amount of sheepishness to make one think she hadn't meant to drag her feet. Her daughter knew better.

"Sorry, darling," she said breathlessly, dropping into a chair. "Your father insisted we drive up to the old Layton estate and couldn't remember the way back." Laughter threaded her words, and she prattled on, "The mansion is in such disrepair. You really should fire that caretaker, Megan. It's a shame to see Daddy's fortune practically rotting away like that."

"I don't have anything to do with the house, you know that." Meg signaled to order and gave it fast. If her mother hadn't shown up when she had, she'd have eaten the table-cloth. "I'm famished. It's been a long day." She observed Alice as she ordered the most expensive dish on the menu and a very dry martini. Her eyes were faintly dark underneath, as if she hadn't gotten enough sleep.

"This is a nice hotel. Not as fine as the ones in Europe, I'll grant you, but nice all the same." Alice tapped a manicured nail on the rim of her glass. "Have you ever considered living at Layton House, Megan?"

"No," she replied honestly. "Grandfather shouldn't have left it to me."

"Hmm. Well, he shouldn't have saddled you with it the way he did. I mean, that clause he had in his will stipulating that you couldn't sell it until you either turned thirty or married . . ."

Meg shrugged and studied her guileless expression carefully. "Arthur takes care of the bills out of the money from the estate holdings. I don't need to go near it. I don't want to."

"You never did like the place, did you?"

"I didn't like the atmosphere. It was oppressive. Grandfather treated the staff like dirt." She shuddered, recalling how harsh he was to everyone in his vicinity.

Alice fingered her chin thoughtfully. "Still, it would be quite the showplace if it were fixed up."

"Let's talk about something else." The food arrived, and Meg listened while Alice told her about the old friends she'd looked up in town and the shopping she'd done. When she stopped to take a breath, Meg jumped in to enquire, "Do you know a man by the name of Fred Reynolds?"

Alice instantly paled but recovered quickly and shook her head. "I don't remember anyone named Fred." The martini disappeared rapidly then, four olives nearly flying across the table when the glass toppled from her unsteady hand. She grabbed a napkin and wiped shaky fingers, her smile not as easy as it was a minute before.

Meg went on alert. Her mother seldom lost her composure, and it was as scary as it was amusing. "He's a doctor. He said he used to know you."

"No, dear, I don't know any Dr. Reynolds," she repeated, annoyed. "How is your fish?"

"Fine."

No one spoke for what seemed like ages. Tired of the game suddenly, Meg asked about something that had bothered her from the moment her parents had contacted her again.

"Why are you and Harry together, Alice?"

"Together? Oh, you mean . . . *well*, I had wanted to surprise you with the news. I'm sure you'll be as excited as we are." The pregnant pause was well-timed, the glitter in her eyes faultless when she announced, "Harry and I have reconciled. We've decided to remarry. Isn't that wonderful?"

Meg felt nauseated.

"I know we didn't get it right the first time," Alice murmured contritely, "but we fully intend to be the parents you deserve from now on." She searched her daughter's face — which had blanched at the word *remarry* — and smiled hugely. "Aren't you going to say anything, Megan?"

Swallowing the lump of cod that had lodged in her throat, Meg muttered, "Congratulations."

"Damn it, Baz! Come down from there," Steven commanded irritably.

The cockatoo sauntered along the edge of the gutter and peered at him. He'd flown out the window and up to the roof half an hour ago and refused to listen to reason.

"It's dark, buddy. You have to come down." Steven scratched his head and tried a different approach. "Please."

Baz puffed out his chest and ignored the plea.

Headlights illuminated the front of the house as Meg pulled in and killed the engine. She joined him directly and stared up at the gutter.

"Do something," he begged, "before the neighbours see us out here and call the landlord."

"They won't care." Her gaze never left the bird.

"Johnny is a mean kid. He knows we can't have pets here."

"I doubt if Johnny is in possession of Rupert's phone number," she dryly stated.

"He'd find it."

"Hmm. What did you do to drive him up there, anyway?"

Steven gasped. "Bazil needs no encouragement to cause trouble. I was working on the computer, and he—"

"So, you weren't paying attention."

"He's a dumb bird, Meg. I vote we take him back."

She shot him a furious glance. "You can't just decide you don't want him because he's a little ornery. Once you took him home he became your responsibility. Grow up!"

Steven sized her up warily, deducing from the closed expression on her face that the evening with her mother had been as disturbing as the rest of their relationship. "How will I deal with him then?"

"Show some interest in his welfare now and again, his happiness. It isn't so hard. Surely a scattered enquiry after his health and such ... his dreams ..." She sighed. "It's a life-long commitment, this parenting thing, not a hobby to pick up and put down like knitting."

"You're rambling. But you're right. I'll be more heedful of Bazil's needs." He watched Meg watching the bird. She didn't seem to be really seeing him, as if her mind was still back at the hotel. "Want to talk about it?"

"Nope."

"Are you sure?"

Sighing, she mumbled, "Maybe later."

Baz eyed them suspiciously as they followed his movements in silence.

"If you don't come down and go inside for the night," Steven called up to him, "we're leaving you out here alone."

The bird twitched his wings as if to shrug.

"He doesn't care," Meg observed.

"No, he doesn't." Then inspiration hit. "You know, sometimes Johnny and his gang whiz by here when trying to beat their curfew," he said casually. "Johnny doesn't have a pet. I'm willing to bet he'd love a big white piece of fluff to annoy his folks with."

Having been present when Steven had regaled Meg with tales of the neighborhood terror, the *fluff* froze.

Meg saw the opening. "You'll have to finish telling me what happened to that little mouse he caught in our yard."

"It's too horrendous to bear repeating. Let me just say, I never knew one tiny rodent could have so much fur until I witnessed the barbaric haircut."

Bazil dropped onto the porch rail and looked longingly toward the front door.

"I do hope Johnny has matured. If not, he's probably graduated to plucking." Steven crossed his arms and smirked as the cockatoo glanced to his left and right, up and down the darkened street.

Meg murmured, "He *must* be gone in for the night by

now. Don't you think?"

Obviously having little or no faith in the surety of Johnny's whereabouts, Baz planted himself directly in Steven's path, so he opened the door.

Some time later, the apartment was quiet so Steven pretended to read a paperback thriller while studying Meg. She sat beside him on the couch flipping through an old photo album impatiently. He watched with growing concern when she desperately scanned the pages, finally reaching the end of the collection a third time before slamming it shut.

"It's bugging me." The comment burst from her with a growl, her slender hands gripping the album anxiously.

"What is?" He gave up attempting to read and laid the book aside. He focused his attention on the woman who so occupied his mind of late that he thought of little else, wishing again that he could erase the troubled expression she seemed to wear constantly since her parents came to visit. The way her eyes grew distant and lost cut right to his heart, and he ached to dispel her worries even as he accepted that she had to deal with them herself.

"All of it," she responded to his gentle question. Wearily, she rubbed her eyes and explained, "I'm getting so many weird vibes from Alice that it's making me paranoid. I feel like I should know the man yet I'm positive I don't."

"Who?"

"Fred Reynolds. That's why I dug out the pictures. I could swear he looks familiar, like I've seen him somewhere. I thought maybe he'd be in an old photograph or something."

Steven took the album from her and leafed through it. "Is it really bothering you that much?"

"I can't describe it. Alice's face tonight when I mentioned his name was the definition of shock. I feel as if she's hiding something. That in itself isn't unusual," she noted wryly, "since she's made a fine art of evasion and artifice for as long as I've been living."

Turning a page, Steven stopped himself from shivering. There, in black and white, was a photo of an older man seated in a wing chair, a silver cane in his gnarled grasp, and he glared imperiously into the camera. His eyes were arctic cold, chin set obstinately. The colorless picture may have hidden the blue eyes of the little girl who sat at his feet, but it could not disguise the sadness there, nor the defeated slump of her thin shoulders beneath the curly mane of hair that he knew would be red.

His jaw throbbed from clenching whilst he slowly scrutinized the reminders that her childhood had been a far cry from his—Meg, standing alone in front of a huge, dark house that he realized must be her grandfather's, her mother posing at the foot of an ornate staircase, her perfect smile plastered on a brittle countenance, her father looking on indifferently as someone snapped a photo.

Not once between the covers of the album did Steven spy one single depiction of Meg and her parents together. And to think he'd ever wondered that she was leery of their motives when they'd turned up out of the blue.

"How hard is it going to be to distract you from the mystery of Dr. Reynolds and whisk you off to bed?" he joked, pulling her close.

"Hmm, let's see." She snuggled into him and offered her ear up for a nibble. "I don't think . . . it'll take . . . too long."

"Oh good." He dragged his mouth along her neck, stopping to place hot kisses as he went. "I find that patience is in short supply when you're around."

"Lucky for me."

"Wanna see who gets luckiest?" he enquired silkily and carried her off to bed.

Hours later, she announced, "I win!"

Sunlight stole across the bed, inching toward the lovers nestled in it, and Meg wondered if she'd ever get used to waking up next to him. Would she awake one morning to discover she'd grown bored with the sensation of his heart beating a slow, steady tattoo against her cheek? Would she be so accustomed to his warm breath fanning her forehead after a while that the idea of missing it would seem absurd? Would the feel of his hair-roughened legs tangled with hers pale in comparison to the smoothness of cotton sheets? She sighed, knowing the answers already.

Sometime between rescuing him from a mugging by certain neighborhood mini-thugs and now, she'd fallen for Steven Kincaid. It could have been when he'd blushed in embarrassment at getting caught in the car door, or perhaps when he'd played the disturbed prospective son-in-law for her parents. But last night, when she'd seen the anger and then compassion in his eyes as he'd looked through her photographs, she'd admitted it to herself. She loved him.

The revelation should have made her happy. Instead, it brought tension to every muscle and halted her breathing momentarily. She waited for the feeling and the man to vanish into thin air. When neither happened, she forced herself to relax slowly, inhaling and exhaling in a relatively normal fashion.

Meg slipped carefully from his embrace, pausing when his arms tightened reflexively before allowing her to slide from beneath the covers. She found her robe and shrugged it on while she left the room, closing the door gently behind her.

Baz was wide awake in the kitchen. She shuffled over to his cage and let him out. He stepped onto her hand and cocked his crested head curiously, sensing her inner turmoil.

"How did I let this happen?" she whispered to him. "It'll

never last. He'll soon realize how lacking I am when it comes to important things. I'll just have to make sure he doesn't find out how I feel. No need suffering that humiliation later on."

Cautiously, the stately bird crept up Meg's arm until he was perched comfortably on her shoulder.

"You don't have a clue what I'm saying, do you?"

Baz touched his cool beak to her face as if in sympathy.

"Exactly what do you mean by that?"

Steven looked askance at his mother—his previously good-natured, roll-with-the-punches mother. "I mean, I don't want to ruin things by bringing up the subject of marriage to Meg," he repeated patiently.

Janey Kincaid's glare was overtly hostile, something the beloved woman rarely was. "Marriage is a wonderful institution. How can a simple discussion ruin things?"

Over the noise in Cass and Caro's back yard, he fought to be heard without drawing Meg's attention. Seeing how engrossed she was playing with a toddler, he said loudly, "Don't sound so insulted. I'm only giving her a little time to adjust."

"Adjust to what? Living in sin?"

"*Mother!*" Steven cringed at her raised voice. "She'll hear you."

"I don't care. If you two aren't serious about each other, I think you should move out of the house." Janey had managed to lower the volume to a medium hiss.

"I can't. My plumbing's been gutted."

"Stay here with your sisters."

Steven laughed until he saw she wasn't amused. "Ma, if you could just meet her family, you'd understand. Meg doesn't believe anyone could want her, much less love her.

She's grown up thinking that. Don't throw a monkey wrench in my carefully planned strategy by mentioning marriage to her," he warned, "or you'll make her nervous."

"She ought to be nervous—living with my son, *out* of wedlock. Imagine what your father will say."

"Don't tell him."

"I don't keep secrets from your father," she huffed indignantly.

"Fine," he agreed, glancing around for a glimpse of Meg through the sea of bodies who'd congregated to stuff their faces with ribs and play touch football. "Just don't tell him until you get home."

Janey stared at her son's love for a while longer. "She likes kids. They like her. Don't take forever getting to the altar. You're no spring chicken." And, so saying, she marched off to get dessert.

Steven groaned. His own mother was reminding him of his advancing age and unwedded state. Well, he'd fix that deplorable situation as soon as possible. That was, if Meg would bend a little.

The lady in question had been quieter than usual all day. After waking to find her side of the bed vacant this morning, he'd been sorely disappointed to discover she'd taken off for the grocery store alone. One of the many things he enjoyed doing with her was loading down the shopping cart with food they didn't need but that he convinced her to try. The afternoon had passed without much communication, and his efforts at drawing her out of her silent mood were met with half smiles and slight shakes of the head.

To add to his growing unease, she'd avoided much physical contact, as well. Every chance he got to touch her he took, but she'd find something to do that removed her from his reach. It was worrisome.

"Are you meditating or trying to burn a hole through

your plate?" Jonas drawled as he sat next to his partner. "You've been frowning at it for a good ten minutes now."

"I like the pattern. It's mesmerizing," he replied thoughtfully.

"Picking out china, are you?"

Steven snorted. "Not at this rate."

The big redhead crunched his beer can. "My, my. Trouble in para —"

"Shut up," was the growled response.

Jonas chuckled meanly. "You want me to beat her up for you?"

"I doubt if she's susceptible to even that brand of persuasion."

"Man, you sound grim." Jonas patted him on the back. "Meg will come around."

"I don't know." He shoved a hand through his hair in frustration. "I thought we were making progress, but today she seems to be backpedaling."

"You picked a stubborn one."

"No more so than you."

Jonas followed his gaze and grinned broadly. Viv grinned back and waddled over to place a lingering kiss on her husband's mouth. She stroked his cheek once and moved on to chat with Eleuthera and Fred. "Worth every second. You'll see."

"Damned right I will," he vowed crossly.

His partner laughed again, then grew sober. "Fred was asking about her."

"Meg?" Steven sat up straighter. "What did he want to know?"

"General stuff. Age, where she went to school, how long you've been seeing her. It was a bit odd." He paused to gauge his friend's reaction. "What's up with that?"

"Hmph. Beats me. Meg went through her photo album

last night trying to find a picture of him. She's positive she must have seen him somewhere before. Maybe when she was a kid."

"Didn't I hear him say he knew her mother?"

Steven nodded. The doctor's attention was again on Meg. Steven tensed as the older man disengaged himself from the group he was conversing with and ambled over to her.

Jonas, who had also watched Fred's nonchalant maneuver, said lowly, "If I didn't already know the man, I'd say he was flirting with a younger woman."

Meg's discomfort waned and disappeared minutes after Fred Reynolds' approach. He chatted amiably, asking about things that she didn't consider too personal. She learned that he used to dabble in art himself and liked to draw caricatures for his younger patients. His easy manner and quick smile were friendly but not overdone. She found herself laughing when he teased the kids at the barbecue and made funny faces, blue eyes twinkling merrily. Soon, he was armed with a large notepad supplied by Caro, doodling for them and delighting even the adults.

Meg joined in at his request, and the two of them spent the next half hour side by side, making pictures and talking about baseball.

"It's so rare to find a woman who appreciates my sense of humor," Fred remarked when the children had scampered off. "Ellie is a gem, but she doesn't get those umpire jokes."

Standing beside him, Eleuthera Mackenzie rolled her eyes expressively. "Basketball jokes are over my head, too. Men and sports. Can't have one without the other."

Meg smiled, liking Fred and his *Ellie* more and more.

CHAPTER EIGHT

"What's up, Meg?"

"Nothing, Steven. Why do you ask?"

"You're too quiet."

"Oh."

The car slowed, and he waited for the light to change. Shooting his passenger a look, he probed, "Fred didn't upset you earlier?"

"No." She kept her head turned to the side window.

"You're not ill, are you?"

"A slight headache."

He edged the car through the intersection and sped up, irritated with her brief replies. A minute later, he tried again. "Tired?"

"Mmm."

"Those kids must have run you ragged."

"Not really."

"The adults then."

"Everybody was nice, Steven."

"Just not your kind of people."

"I don't blend in with any particular *kind*."

He ground his teeth.

"Cut that out," she ordered absently.

"What?"

"You're grinding. You do that in your sleep."

"Keep you awake?"

"As a matter of fact—"

"'Cause if it does, I can—"

" —it does."

Steven exhaled slowly, forcing his fingers to surrender their white-knuckled grip on the wheel. "Does it really?"

Meg nodded once.

"I'll sleep in my room tonight."

No reply.

"Baz will keep me company. We can discuss getting him a mate . . . or an amped-up SUV. Maybe a plane. He'd like that, don't you think?"

Silence.

Tires squealed as he tore into the driveway, throwing Meg off balance. Feeling very ungentlemanly, he cut the ignition and got out, not bothering to wait for her. The apartment was dark when he stalked through it and to his room. Two could play this game.

He slammed the door and stretched out on his bed facing it. He'd give it three minutes before she came in and apologized. Five minutes . . . ten.

The sounds coming from the kitchen a half hour later told him she didn't plan on expressing her remorse any time soon. The clink of a coffee cup meant it was going to be a long interval.

This was childish, a grown man playing games because he was miffed. Janey had taught him better. But Janey hadn't told him what to do about Meg.

He sat up and listened when her footsteps sounded down the hall and past his door, hesitating only a fraction, then she continued on to her own room.

Cursing softly, Steven went to get some coffee, knowing he wouldn't be able to sleep if he tried. The light on her house phone was blinking, and he stopped beside it, debating whether or not to play the messages. Meg either hadn't been interested in them or she hadn't remembered to check. They could be for him . . . or not. He'd be invading her privacy if he played them in her absence. But they *could* be for him. He hovered his hand over the button then dropped it to his side.

"Let her check her own friggin' messages."

A rustling noise behind him broke the stillness of the kitchen. Baz peered out from his cage next to the window.

"You should consider yourself lucky, buddy. Stay single. Women are trouble."

His captive audience tilted his head toward the hallway.

"I know what you're thinking," Steven muttered morosely. "You want me to go talk to her, make nice, be understanding because she's confused. Well, I'm confused, too, and she's not making nice with me."

Baz glowered at him.

"You are a stuck-up bird, did you know that? Always looking down that big, black nose at people, preening like a peacock."

Baz turned on his perch and showed the human his back.

"Fine, ignore me. Everyone else does." He tossed what remained of the coffee in the sink and rinsed his cup, trying to figure out what he'd done to bring about the change in Meg's attitude. Between yesterday and this morning, all he'd done was talk to her about her parents, made love with her, talked about little stuff as they laid in bed, made love with her — that was it! He straightened from his slouched position so fast he nearly got whiplash. Meg had grown tired of him.

"Already? She got her fill and now the thrill is gone — *already?*" The idea was more than depressing, but it made sense . . . and it ticked him off big time.

After knocking on Meg's door and getting no answer, he restrained himself sufficiently to ease it open instead of barging in. His vision adjusted to the darkness, his gaze going to the huddled form in the bed. He wavered, remembering she'd had a headache. Perhaps she'd taken something for it and had gone to sleep. The anger that was left faded, to be replaced with a tenderness he hadn't known he'd possessed before meeting her.

Moving closer, he questioned his right to be upset and decided he really didn't have one. If a few nights was all she wanted—who was he kidding to think he was entitled to more? After all, he'd practically bulldozed his way into her life, disregarding her claim of preferring to stay uninvolved and alone.

On the other hand, he mused, she'd let him closer than any other man and had given him one of the most precious gifts a woman could give. She'd been warm and passionate, responding to every overture since that first night together with both affection and intense desire. Could her ardor have cooled so fast? Literally overnight?

"Meg?" he whispered softly, wanting to ask but loathe to disturb her. He reached down and traced the fullness of her bottom lip, drawing away when she stirred in her sleep and relaxed again.

Steven argued with himself over the wisdom of his actions only a moment before he undressed and slipped beneath the blankets. Concerned that she might wake up, he gingerly placed an arm around her waist and cuddled in, spoon-fashion behind her, inhaling the delicate scent of her hair as he settled down. She didn't move or give any sign that she was conscious, and minutes later he slid into a light slumber, leaving his question unanswered for another day.

Meg pressed against the hand cupping her breast, smiling dreamily while the intimate cloak of pleasure drifted around her. Steven's breath tickled the back of her neck, each respiration matching her own.

Steven.

She'd virtually snubbed him all day, encouraging the rotten mood that had been in evidence when they'd left the barbecue. While her manners had proved perfect—annoyingly so—her behaviour was still as sour as lemon juice. If she'd wanted to put him off, she had in spades. But apparently, he had an even more forgiving nature than she suspected if the feel of his strong arms and rampant erection were any indication. Even in sleep he was amorous. She smiled tenderly, unable to deny the man was endearing.

And rock hard.

Arching her back, she pushed against him, gratified when she detected the change in his breathing pattern. He groaned and returned the pressure, and her satin teddy was too thin to disguise the magnitude of his arousal.

"Cut it out, Meggie," he grated, "or I might forget how badly you don't want this."

Shocked rigid, Meg gasped, "I don't?"

"You've been giving me the freeze ever since we woke up this morning. Rather, since you ran off to the grocer's and left me to wake up *alone*." Although his swollen shaft was still crowding her behind, his arm was tight, restricting her titillating wiggles. "If you grew bored with having me around that fast you could have told me," he muttered.

"I'm not bored with you. How could you think I was bored?"

He snorted. "Gee, suddenly I can't get more than one sentence out of you at a time, you can't stand to let me touch you—"

Meg finally achieved a wiggle.

"—and ... uh ... damn."

"If you assumed I didn't want you, why get in bed with me naked? Did you think I wouldn't notice?"

"Stop that shimmying, minx."

"This?"

"Meg," he ground out, "don't be a tease."

"All right." With a swift twist of her body, she pinned him against the mattress, hands on his hard shoulders. He caught her by the hips, and she settled on him, rubbing him slowly. "No teasing."

Steven's eyes were half closed, and he followed her deliberate motions—the way she let the straps of her teddy slide from her shoulders, the barely perceptible sway of her breasts as she uncovered them. Her glorious hair fell like a curtain around him when she leaned forward to place one eager nipple in his mouth. He suckled greedily and urged her higher, taking her other breast in turn and lavishing it with the same treatment. Sensual heat shot through her when he alternated from one pebbled tip to the other. The grip she had on his shoulders loosened, and the feeling threatened to overpower her.

Seizing the elusive fiber that remained of her control, she freed herself and moved lower, trailing hot kisses down his face and neck to his chest. There, she caressed him the same way, scraping her teeth across his nipples and flicking her tongue to assuage the abrasion. He guided her mouth back to his and took her sigh of delight as his own, bringing her fully onto him.

"Steven." Meg levered her body away slightly and wedged a hand between them and down, taking his silky length in her grasp.

He tried to stop her, whispering his need to be inside her, but she quieted him with slow kisses and even slower strokes. Chest heaving and glistening with a fine sheen of perspiration, the strain of withholding his release was indisputable with every clenched muscle she touched. She knew he held back as much for her enjoyment as his, but she also knew he wouldn't stand much more.

"Enough," he gritted seconds later, flipping her onto her

back.

He ripped the fabric from her hips, and she didn't care that it was ruined, only that he would soon be where she ached to feel him, pulsing within her.

Steven knelt and pulled her legs around him, driving his erection into her molten center. No sooner had he buried himself than he withdrew and rammed into her again, pumping in a powerful rhythm that she gladly kept pace with, all the time reveling in the fire lighting his eyes. She was spellbound when he rose up, tilting her hips and grinding against her fervently, repeating the motion until she exploded into a million tiny shards of rapture. Gaze still locked with Meg's, he gave one deep thrust, then another, and spilled his seed, hot and sweet inside her.

Boneless bliss radiated through Meg while she cradled him to her, absorbing the sensation of his weakened body giving over to sleep. His weight was secure and comforting, and she welcomed it as she followed him into unconsciousness, thinking what it would be like to hold him this way forever.

"Wake up, Meggie," the raspy voice persisted. The heated body it came from blanketed hers like a vibrant, sensual shield, pressing her into the soft bed. Steven's chest created a unique friction on her nipples, stirring her passion all over. "We need to talk."

"No," she moaned. "No talking." She kissed his neck, distracting him long enough to slip her hands around to his tight behind.

"Forget it." He rolled to the side and pinned her legs beneath one of his. Propped on an elbow, he announced from his dominant position, "While making love to you at any time is an experience best described as splendidly superb, it's not a good idea to try to use it as a substitute for verbal communication."

The lamp glared ghoulishly in her eyes when he reached across to flip it on.

Squinting, Meg protested, "I thought we communicated very well . . . and we were very verbal about it."

Steven sighed and scratched his bristly chin. "Don't be cute. You know what I mean. What's troubling you?"

"Nothing."

"If ever a lie did cross your delectable lips—"

"All right!" She frowned at the wall in an attempt to elude his discerning look. "I woke up this morning—yesterday morning—feeling very uncomfortable with this situation."

"Uncomfortable how?"

"Just overwhelmed, I guess." Plucking edgily at the comforter, she went on, "Then, to make matters worse, your mother was sending me these furious glares at the barbecue. I feel as if I'm disappointing your entire family because I don't fit in."

"Good Lord, Meg. You nestled in with the Kincaid clan like a piece of the puzzle no one knew was missing. My sisters adore you, my parents want to take you home with them and fatten you up. Heck, my partner's mother would like nothing better than to adopt you." He cupped her chin so that she had to look at him. "I think there's something you're not telling me."

Meg swallowed the lump that had risen in her throat. "Your mother doesn't think I'm good enough for you," was what came out of her mouth. Her eyes stung unexpectedly when she realized it was true. Not only had her newly discovered love for Steven been on her mind, but she'd worried on some deep level that his family wouldn't approve of her.

"Sweetheart, that isn't true, and you know it. In some respects, Janey is more liberal than one would expect, but in others she's really old-fashioned. She's not quite happy with the *common-law* notion, that's all."

"Are you sure?"

"Trust me, she's almost as taken with you as I am."

Meg sniffed, trying to stop the tears from spilling. "How taken is that?"

"You mean, you don't know?" Steven rolled them both until she lay atop him. Brushing her fiery hair back, his clear green gaze on hers, he said, "I love you."

Meg returned his kiss hungrily, heedless that she was crying silently. When she raised her head, she was stunned to find that his eyes were also shiny. "No one's ever told me that before," she haltingly whispered.

"Then I'll have to make sure you hear it often. Starting now."

As their bodies merged once more, he murmured to her over and over how much he adored her, wanted her. All through the night he kissed her tears away, replacing them with smiles and sighs of pleasure.

When the sun crept into the room, one tiny part of her believed that he really did love her.

"Whatcha doin', Mr. Kinket?"

Steven groaned and peered over his shoulder, the rake in his hand held defensively to ward off a rock or any type of debris the toothless terror might find accessible. "Raking the grass."

"Oh. Are ya gonna stuff it in those?" Johnny asked, tossing his head at the garbage bags on the bottom step.

Both the front and back yards were freshly mowed and had only one mound of grass apiece to be collected. Unless Johnny decided to play. That had resulted in re-raking once before.

Thinking fast, Steven replied blandly, "Actually, I was going to spread it over the lawn again."

"Why?"

"Mulch."

"What's that?"

"It's a kind of natural fertilizer."

Johnny frowned. "Then what didja cut it in the first place for if you were gonna put it back?"

"Uh, it has to die so it can rot. Yeah. So I had to cut it."

"Oh." Pause. "So what're the bags for?"

Jeez. "Collecting garbage around the yard."

"So, you fertilize the lawn with rotted stuff and pick up the garbage after?"

"Pretty much."

"Cool." Johnny grinned and raced off to his house.

Steven sighed gratefully at his rapid departure. After a nearly sleepless night making love with Meg, he had no energy left to chase the neighborhood demon from the property. It was a good thing his curiosity had been curbed so easily. One minor fib, and he didn't have to shell out five bucks to make the kid disappear. He chuckled at his own little joke.

Humor died a vicious death when he returned from getting a cold drink to discover that Johnny had very creative skills of interpretation.

The lawn was littered with kitchen refuse. Everything from banana peels to tin cans had been scattered about, courtesy of Johnny. He stood shaking out two white plastic bags, making certain that every last morsel of mang was emptied.

"There you go, Mr. Kinket. Whatever won't rot you can put in the bags when you go around!"

"I'm not sure," Meg said into the phone as the front door banged. She surveyed Steven's scowl and mouthed, "Your mother."

"Well, since your parents are here, and Jon and I are here, we may as well all get together."

Janey's suggestion would have seemed perfectly natural in any case but this one. Unfortunately, trying to explain that her own parents weren't exactly normal was discomfiting for Meg, so in the end she didn't bother.

"I'll see if they're free this evening."

Steven quirked an eyebrow from across the kitchen.

"Good," Janey approved. "We're looking forward to meeting them. Tell my son to wear a tie. Bye now!"

Meg hung up and cringed. "Your mother is very persistent. We may be having dinner with Alice and Harry . . . in a restaurant—all six of us."

"Oh Lord."

"What are we supposed to do?" The very idea of sitting through a meal with his parents while hers behaved as they usually did made her queasy.

"We'll go, of course." Steven's face was the picture of innocence, but she suspected he'd had a hand in Janey extending the invitation.

"You can't be serious. My flighty mother and uninterested father will make things very unpleasant. I don't want to go."

"It's just one little dinner, Meg." He smirked. "I feel as if I've said that before. How bad can it be?"

Alice and Harry were late, of course, the reason being that the chauffeur had driven them to Rocky's Restaurant instead of Rosa's. Seeing as how Rocky's was a sports bar, Meg was quite certain that Harry had been responsible for the misdirection.

Steven took it upon himself to make introductions, and she was grateful as her jaw was already aching from the tension. When everyone was seated and polite comments exchanged about the cozy Italian restaurant, he slid a hand beneath the table and patted her clenched ones reassuringly. It was a comforting gesture, but it buoyed her spirits only a fraction. The evening had just begun.

"So, Alice," Steven commenced into the silence, "how are you enjoying your stay?"

"Oh, it's been absolutely marvelous," she responded, looking at him warily. "It's a shame we haven't got together more often. I trust you're feeling better?"

"Oh, definitely. Those little spells tend to come and go." He shrugged offhandedly in his parents' direction and gave them a look that said *Ask me later.*

Meg gulped her wine . . . twice.

"You don't live in St. John's?" Janey enquired of the Laytons, her genuine smile inviting a rambling reply from Alice, who complained that the air was bad for her skin and the people too *local*.

"Oh. You must visit a lot then, what with Meg here."

"When we can squeeze it in," Alice lied easily. "Unfortunately, Harry is so busy with business these days that we rarely have time."

"What business are you in?" Jon slipped in congenially to Meg's father.

"I'm an investor. Real estate." Harry proceeded to extol the fine points of a deal he'd recently made, stopping short of soliciting Jon's financial participation by saying, "We're always looking for interested parties to join in."

"Isn't that a coincidence, Steven?" Janey exclaimed laughingly. "You'll have to compare notes with Harry about your investments." To Alice, she remarked, "He's got a fine talent for the stock market. Jon and I have benefitted greatly from his advice."

"Really?" Alice turned her suddenly rapt gaze to Steven, completely missing her ex and future husband's stony expression.

Meg saw it and wondered why he'd frozen so quickly. She also saw that her glass was empty and nudged her date for a refill. He complied, though frowningly.

"Where did you say this real estate was?" Steven prodded a scrap or two more from Harry about his big deal before they were all presented with plates of steaming pasta and more wine.

By the time dessert was consumed, Meg had a fuzzy head. Her upper body was weaving to and fro, and she tried to count the glasses of wine on her fingers under cover of the tablecloth.

"You're on your fifth."

She blinked at Steven and hissed, "Why didn't you stop me?"

"You damn near took a chunk out of my leg when you pinched me."

"Oh. Sorry."

Suitably inebriated for the argument that soon erupted over who paid the bill, she nonetheless let out a feeble cry of distress. Harry pompously insisted on paying since he was far better off and was not deterred by the dull flush that rose in Jon Kincaid's face at the insult. He wasn't even aware of it as Janey began chattering rapidly to divert her husband's attention and soothe his wounded ego. Jon continued the debate until he noticed the look of horrified humiliation Meg wore and must have decided to take pity on her.

Breathing a sigh of relief that she suspected was premature, Meg carefully hung on to Steven's arm, and they waited for their car to be brought around.

Alice touched her cheek in a gentle fashion and told her to come by the hotel the next day. Her hand dropped when she realized she had no audience and she smiled vacantly, her gaze darting around the foyer. A patron coming in stopped her cold, one hand going to her throat when the distinguished man spoke to Janey and Jon in a friendly manner and turned his gray head to bestow a curt nod upon her. He then went inside with Eleuthera Mackenzie on his arm.

The pallor of her mother's face did not go unnoticed by Steven, his glance tracking Fred Reynolds narrowly as he disappeared.

"I would like to say that they aren't usually so offensive but I'd be lying." The careful declaration escaped Meg's partially numbed lips once the four of them were in the Kincaid's sedan. Her parents had ordered the limo back to the hotel, not wanting to be mashed in the back seat.

"No worries, dear," Janey cheerfully told her. "As they say, if you don't have a strange relative or two in your family, chances are you're it."

Steven kissed the top of her head and pulled her close on the seat. She hiccupped all the way home.

For a drunk woman she moved pretty fast.

He'd only gone back outside to return some photos to his mother and bid them goodnight. Three minutes, tops. Yet she was already sipping from another wineglass, the half-empty bottle on the kitchen counter.

"It was in da *fridge*." She stared at him stubbornly. "Left from the other night. 'Member?"

"Yes, I remember."

"Wansome?"

"No, and you've had enough." He took the glass and set it aside.

Meg burped and swayed. "It'll hep me seep."

"I could have given you something for that," he replied suggestively.

Woozy, she smiled. "You can still gimme that."

"Uh-uh." Steven picked her up and strode to her room. "You're too drunk."

"So?"

"I'd be taking advantage."

"Iss not like we haven't dunnit aw-ready."

Lowering her limp body to the bed, he quickly undressed her. "It wouldn't be any fun for you."

"Hmph! Wanna bet?" She grabbed his tie and pulled him down for a wine-sweetened kiss. "I'm having tons of fun," she murmured throatily.

Sidetracked by the sight of her red curls fanned out on the pillow, he had to concentrate that much harder while disengaging her hold on the tie. That finally accomplished, he dodged her as she went for his belt. "Stop that. My mother raised me better."

Meg pouted, her big blue eyes drifting closed when she let him cover her with a blanket. They shot open when he made the mistake of leaning over to plump her pillow, and she snatched the opportunity—along with his shirt—in both hands.

"You'll be the death of me yet," he grumbled, sitting next to her and patiently waiting for her to rid him of his clothes. Bare-chested now, he complained, "You won't respect me in the morning."

Meg kissed him again, and he forgot how noble he was.

"I left the condoms," he gasped, "in the bathroom drawer."

"There's some in the nightstand." Her hands were busy inside his pants.

"No . . . there isn't. They're all gone."

"Mmm. Hurry up," she said, giving him a shove toward the door.

Almost tripping with his pants around his ankles, he shuffled out to the bathroom, kicking them free as he went.

The new box of protection eluded his reach when he rummaged through the drawer, and he cursed under his breath. The pressure inside his briefs was explosive, and his forehead beaded with sweat while he fought to ignore the agony. At last, his hand closing on the condoms, he bolted back to the bedroom.

Meg was snoring softly, one hand flung to the side, the other loosely clutching the blanket over her chest. Her cheeks still flushed from a mixture of desire and wine, she was sound asleep.

Steven let the box drop to the floor and took in a deep breath, planting his hands on his hips and scowling downward at his throbbing arousal. As his stiff-as-a-board erection continued to strain against his underwear, he muttered, "Oh, give it a rest."

A thousand miniature jack hammers pounded Meg's brain, drilling holes everywhere she'd ever had a thought. Her eyes were thankfully glued shut against the light pouring in from outside, the lids like sandpaper on her eyeballs.

"Steven?" The croak emerged from her dry mouth hopefully. When no response came from his side of the bed, she cautiously moved an arm in search of another body. Her hand met air and cotton sheets.

No Steven.

She whimpered and eased onto her back, holding her head in place. Dimly, she wondered why she felt so miserable, then winced as the evening before flashed back — her parents, his parents, the wine, the restaurant, the wine, Fred Reynolds, the wine . . .

How could she let herself get drunk? She never got drunk.

The jack hammers sped up when the phone on the

nightstand whirred loudly. She swiped at the receiver and waited for the room to stop spinning before she hung it up again without saying a word. She didn't think she could talk until the wool was washed out of her mouth.

Managing to pry one eye open, she spotted the note in Steven's handwriting. Plucking it from the stand, she read.

Gone to work. Stay in bed. Call you later — Steven. PS: Love you.

She smiled, albeit grimly.

The phone started anew, but this time she put it to her ear, expecting it to be him.

"H'lo?"

"Megan? Megan Layton, is that you?" asked a reedy voice.

"Yes?"

"My darling girl, I've been trying to reach you."

"Arthur?" A picture of the aging attorney materialized in Meg's mind, and she sat up slowly, the fog penetrated by the urgency of his tone. "Is everything okay?"

He harrumphed grouchily, a habit he had whether he was grouchy or not. "That depends on who you ask. I've heard from your so-called family."

"Oh, yes. They're here in St. John's."

"What? Already?"

"I'm afraid so. Has something happened with the estate?" Meg was hoping vaguely for a fire or termites.

"No, no," came the disappointing answer. "They contacted me a few weeks ago, poking around about the validity of your grandfather's will. Now, listen here, Megan, don't you go along with them. The inheritance — as much as you despise it — is rightfully yours. Niles would roll over in his grave if he knew Harry was about to move in there. As for the money, he left enough to those two for a dozen lifetimes."

"Arthur, what's going on?" An old sinking sensation, the most familiar when it came to dealing with her parents, rose up and threatened to suffocate Meg. Alice's voice asking about Layton House echoed in her ears, for a moment drowning out the one on the phone.

" —money," Arthur was saying angrily. "Spent the whole damned lot, they did. Can you imagine? *Every last dime!*"

The hangover haze evaporated instantly. She fumbled for something to say — anything that wouldn't come out in frantic, incoherent fragments. Her stunned mouth opened and closed again, emitting no sound.

"Megan? Megan, are you still there?"

"Ah . . . yes, Arthur. Still here." Her heart rate calmed a little, and she put forth the hesitant question, "Do you mean they're broke?"

"As china on the pantry floor."

"But what about Harry's investments, this big deal he's been talking about?"

"A get-rich-quick scheme. A scam. Don't give him a penny, Megan. Not the house either." Arthur's last words accompanied a wheeze, and he hacked dryly before he went on. "They've spent millions of their own inheritance and now they're after yours."

Meg was overcome with a fatalistic stillness. That explained the recent interest in her whereabouts. Once again, Alice and Harry were being — well, Alice and Harry.

"Thank you for the warning, Arthur."

"Dear girl," he sighed, "I've always felt you deserved better. Niles was a pompous, domineering ass, and his offspring and her choice of husband were just as bad. I often wished Alice had married that nice . . . well, never mind. I only wished you were happy."

"Don't worry about me, Arthur. I could always take care of myself." Then, smiling sadly, she cradled the phone.

CHAPTER NINE

"What are you doing?" Jonas poked his head into Steven's office and eyed the paper chaos on the desk. "I thought you'd be finished for the day."

"Yeah," he muttered. "I got caught up in something." Shuffling printouts and faxes, he motioned for his partner to close the door. "Have you ever heard of a development called Tropical Acres in the Bahamas?"

Stretching back in a chair, Jonas considered the question for a minute. "Can't say I have. Why?"

"Harry Layton claims he has a small island that he's developing with an elite consortium of investors. Tropical Acres is supposedly a resort in the making on said island."

"But?"

Steven blew out a frustrated sigh. "I haven't been able to find a record of the planned resort or contact anyone as an investor. I'm waiting on a fax from the tourism department to determine the location of Harry's overly lauded *Kolamanga*."

"You think it's a con?"

"I think it's possible. While Harry never worked for or did business with his father-in-law, he may have taken a page from old Niles' book." He rolled his shoulders, grimacing at the stiffness there. "Meg's parents have put her through enough. I hope they aren't trying to drag her into some illegal scheme they've concocted."

"They wouldn't, would they? Involve their own daughter, I mean." The redhead narrowed his eyes when Steven just looked at him. "They would?"

"Alice and Harry are perpetually preoccupied with money and all the good things in life—except the one thing in their lives that's really worth anything."

"Meg," Jonas surmised.

"Mmm. I've yet to meet two people so indifferent toward their only child." A black expression appeared on Steven's face as he thought about the Laytons' neglect. If it weren't for their disgraceful treatment of Meg, she wouldn't feel so unloved and unlovable. Instead, she had a helluva time believing he cared for her as he did and hadn't admitted to any depth of feeling for him thus far.

The fax machine beeped and whirred to life. Both men stood, scanning over the message it delivered.

Cursing succinctly, Steven tore the paper off and read it a second time out loud. "'No *Kolamanga* in existence in the Bahamas nor any other island group with this same geographical description.'"

"Seems like Harry is up to Niles' old tricks," Jonas murmured thoughtfully.

"And I'm wondering if he's been up to them before this." He balled up the fax and tossed it in the trash. "I think I'll call JJ and have him find out."

JJ Vanzant was both efficient and fast and only needed an hour to obtain the information for his friend. Over the phone, he rattled off a list of previous *investments* Harry had set up. "The man is in debt to three different foreign governments plus his own. He's even wanted in England on extortion charges."

"Wonderful," was Steven's sarcastic comment. "I suppose he has no way to pay off these debts?"

"Uh-uh. Not a wooden nickel."

"And his ex-wife?"

"Very little. She owes money to no less than six banks. I

don't know how she managed that one." JJ sounded baffled and rang off with the promise to send over the documentation in the morning.

"Damn them both," grumbled Steven. "It's a safe bet they're after Meg's inheritance."

"What now? Are you going to tell her?" Jonas followed him to the elevators.

"I have to. How am I supposed to tell her she was right from the beginning — that her parents are here because they want something from her? Even though she suspected that when they showed up, it'll hurt her just the same." He didn't say that he feared she would pull away from him when she found out, but he knew that was exactly how she would react.

Meg rapped on the door to her parents' suite for a third time. Her sneakered foot beat an angry cadence on the carpet, and she listened to the scuffling noises from within. Finally, the door slowly opened. and a bleary-eyed Alice grabbed for the handle as Meg barreled past.

"What on earth are you doing here at this hour?" her mother asked in a scratchy voice. She yawned and ran a hand over spiky blonde hair.

"It's after six. Where's Harry?" Meg looked around the sitting area with a wry twist of the mouth. Empty gin and vodka bottles were on the table, dirty dishes, no doubt left for housekeeping from the night before. The place was a mess considering it *had* housekeeping staff.

"Still in bed." Alice tried a coquettish smile. "We had quite a celebration last night. Your father's real estate deal is coming along smashingly. I felt a drink or two was in order."

"Toasting the poor suckers who sank their hard-earned

money into his scam?" She stared at her mother's gaping mouth and the alarm flickering across her face. "Yes, I know all about it."

Nervously, Alice erupted in a tittering laugh. "I don't know what you mean, dear."

"I had a long talk with Arthur this morning. He was very informative about a few things."

"That old coot!" Alice scoffed, "He's senile, for heaven's sake. Your father's deal is perfectly legitimate and extremely lucrative." She strode to the mini-bar and sloshed some gin into a glass. Gulping the liquid down, she turned back to Meg. "Arthur is a miser who can't stand to let loose the purse strings to Daddy's fortune. He's a vindictive rat, Megan. Surely, you don't believe his lies?"

"Are they lies? Because it won't take much to find out," she cautioned when it appeared Alice was ready for another creative fabrication.

"Harry is very good with his investments." Her mother gnawed a lip as if trying to decide how best to divulge the next tidbit. "But once or twice . . . well, not everything works the way one plans and — "

"And one ends up owing money *they* can't repay." Meg flopped onto a sofa, shaking her head. "Pretty soon, they're seeking investors for a big project out in the boonies, sight unseen and raking in money to cover huge debts. But somehow, even that money doesn't get where *one* intends for it to go and it gets spent." She laughed humourlessly. "That sounds old hat, Alice. I believe I read it in a newspaper article years ago. Only then, it referred to my grandfather's shenanigans."

"Megan, darling, it isn't all that bad. We've just had a bad run of it lately." That was as close to whining as her mother ever came. Joining Meg on the sofa, she said petulantly, "With a little help we'll be on our feet again."

"*We?*"

"Me and Harry. You didn't think that paltry sum of money Daddy left me would last, did you? Goodness, that couldn't keep me in the manner to which I became accustomed growing up. I had to contact your father and find a way to make more."

Meg paled. "Then it really is gone? You succeeded in squandering millions of dollars in a few short years?"

"Well, really, a couple years in Vegas, a palimony suit here and there—it can go very quickly without one even realizing it."

"If *you* could stand to be sensible," Meg gritted, "*you* would have lived to a ripe old age in the lap of luxury."

Alice lifted a shoulder negligently. "It's understandable. I mean, the stress of being pregnant and married so young did take its toll. You were such a handful." Her ringed hands smoothed the barely noticeable lines beside her eyes, accentuating their presence. "I don't see why you'd object to helping your parents out a little. You don't even touch Daddy's money, and it's only right after all we went through to raise you."

Vivid reflections came to life for Meg. Superimposed over her mother's guileless expression, they came and went like a slide show.

Her fifth birthday had passed at Layton House as she'd sat alone and blew out the candles, wishing her mother wasn't off to Italy while the house staff sang *Happy Birthday*. Arthur was there, trying to appear excited while darting impatient glances toward the closed door of the den where Harry was closeted with a bottle of scotch. Her grandfather was in South America checking out a property, also conspicuously absent.

Seven-year-old feet the dance instructor claimed floated on air turned to lead at the all-important recital. She'd scanned the audience for endless minutes before the curtain went up and saw only two empty seats where her parents had promised to be. Perversely, she'd been thankful for their absence while tears streamed down her face through the number she'd practiced to death with the class, automatically following steps so that she didn't embarrass the other girls with a clumsy mistake.

"Where are you going, Mommy?" her ten-year-old self echoed from the doorway of her mother's room as she'd packed her cases. "Can I come this time?" she'd timidly asked, not knowing there would be no return trip.

She'd searched the sea of faces again from the podium of her high school graduation. Alice had been gone for years by then, but Meg had always hoped her father would remember to be there. Disappointed once more, she'd defiantly delivered a rousing valedictory speech and had been congratulated by every parent but her own.

College graduation . . . her first sale to a magazine . . .

"Megan! Pay attention to me!"

Ignoring Alice's command, she left the sofa and went to the window overlooking the harbor. "Yes, *Mother*," she choked in a whispery voice, "you've done so much for me. It's time I showed how grateful I am."

"I knew you'd agree to help Harry and I just this once." Alice drifted over and made a bungling attempt at hugging her. Sensing the rigid set of her body, she pulled back and stared at Meg enquiringly.

"Trust me, Alice, you'll never have to worry about money for as long as you live. Not you or Harry. There is one thing I want, though."

"Anything, dear. What is it?" Her mother's eyes fair shone with glee.

"We'll discuss it once I've made some arrangements."

The last thing she heard as she left the suite was Alice

bursting into the other room to share news of their good fortune with Harry.

"I'm sorry, Steven, I have not seen her in days." Olaf's rumbling reply sent another shiver of apprehension up his spine.

"Is there anyone else I can call?" He pinched the bridge of his nose, trying in vain to wish away the ache surrounding it. "What about your girlfriend?"

"No, no. Fannie is here. She says she has not seen Meg either. Have you had a fight with her?" the Nordic giant demanded.

"No, I swear."

"Hmm. How long has she been missing?"

Clenching the receiver until his knuckles hurt, he repeated, "I don't know. I came home from work hours ago, and she was gone. No message, no phone call, nothing."

"She's a big girl, Steven. If she managed to stay out of trouble before you moved in on her —"

"*With* her."

" — then she'll do the same now."

Exasperated, Steven sighed and said loudly, "It's almost midnight. I don't know where she is."

Olaf chuckled. "Calm down. I'm sure she is fine."

"You're no help, you fiend." He hung up and grabbed the phone book.

Fifteen minutes later, he dropped the receiver and told Baz, "At least she hasn't checked into a hospital." He'd called all of them and the police to see if there had been any accidents. His worry bordered on panic now as he glanced at his watch. "Twelve-o-two. This is awfully inconsiderate of your mistress," he informed the caged cockatoo. "Aren't women supposed to be the more sensitive sex?"

Headlights flashed across the wall just then, and he practically flew to the door and threw it wide. "Where the hell have you been?!"

Meg didn't cast a peek his way. Brushing by him, she tossed her keys on the counter. "Out driving."

"To Australia? Why didn't you call?" he groused, ignoring the resentful tilt of her chin. "Do you know I've been worried sick?"

She pretended not to hear and proceeded to free Baz and get him a drink.

"Are you going to answer me, or do I have to start pulling fingernails?" Steven stood, feet braced, and scowled darkly at her. He deserved to know what she'd been doing after pacing a hole in the floor, didn't he? He'd imagined all sorts of horrible fates had happened to her in the hours since returning home. "Meg?"

"What? What is it?" she asked sourly and whirled to face him. Her eyes were rimmed with red, the broken look in them intolerable.

"You've been crying." His anger drained away immediately. In its place came a dreadful sense of foreboding mixed with compassion. "You know about Harry's deal."

Shrugging bitterly, she exclaimed, "Harry's deal, Harry's other deals, Alice's deal with Harry. I'd be stupid not to know, wouldn't I?" She avoided his attempt to pull her near and batted his hands testily. "Leave me alone. You probably realized Harry was a criminal even before he opened his mouth about that damned *Kolamanga!* But did I, stupid little Megan? No. Do you know why? Because even after all these years I still hold on to that tiny shred of hope that my parents will come to me because I'm their daughter and not because they need someone to bail them out of a *deal!*" she screamed. Her blue eyes swam with tears and spilled over, but still she held him off. "And who are you, anyway, to want to know where I've been? My whereabouts are none of your concern!"

Steven prodded softly, "Are you done?"

"No." She scrubbed her wet cheeks and sniffed inelegantly. "Where's Baz?"

"He fled when you began yelling."

"I'm not yelling," she said loud enough that he flinched.

"We need to talk, Meg."

"No, we don't. Not about where I've been and not about my screwy family. It's none . . . of . . . your . . . business. My *life* is none of your business."

"The hell it isn't," he shouted. "We're involved big time whether you like it or not. I'm not letting you shut me out, Meg."

"Too bad. Get your things together and leave." So calmly did she say it that he wondered if he'd heard wrong or was losing his mind. "Now."

"You can't be serious." But he saw that she was and tried again to reach out to her. She scooted around him and headed for his room. "What are you doing?"

"Helping you pack."

"I'm not leaving."

"Yes, you are." Meg hauled his suitcase from the closet and threw it on the bed. "My life was fine till you decided to drop into it."

"I was here first, remember?" He blocked her access to the dresser.

"Then you should have stayed on your side of the wall."

"We're lovers now. You can't just kick me out."

"We had sex. It was fantastic, more than fantastic, but just *sex*."

His head reared as if she'd slapped him, and he felt the sting of her words. "I love you," he growled in her face. He wagged a finger in warning when she tried to object. "Right now you need space and time to calm down. I'll give it to you . . . but I'll be back."

"I don't want you to come back."

"Tough," he told her, stuffing a small overnight case with clothes.

Meg folded her arms mutinously. "I mean it. You may as well pack it all."

Slinging his laptop over one shoulder, he bent and kissed her soundly. "When you're thinking clearly —"

"I am."

" — you can find me."

"Goodbye, Steven," she said quietly.

He stared at the top of her head for a moment and then turned to go. Before he shut the outer door, he called out, "We're not finished!" When he got no response, he left.

A buzzing started in her ears after he was gone, and she realized it was only silence. She'd been surrounded by it before he'd steamrolled his way into her life. Why did it sound so foreign, so empty now?

Wandering despondently back to the kitchen, she paused beside the clock on the wall. The hands moved with no sound, and she thought how odd it was that she'd bought the thing because it didn't tick. Now it only added to the maddening quiet in the apartment.

Had Steven really been here long enough to alter the atmosphere? Was his presence the reason every morning had seemed to pulse with activity and every night had been enhanced with the knowledge that another person was sharing her space? That was ridiculous. She *liked* her space — lots of it — alone. Like now.

A tapping noise came from behind her. She turned to find the only other occupant of her space looking up at her warily.

"I won't bite, Baz. You can come out."

He glanced at the front door and back at his mistress.

"Yes," Meg sighed, "he's gone. I don't need him anyway. I don't need anyone." She sniffed and swallowed convulsively. "I knew Steven Kincaid was trouble the first time I laid eyes on him. I definitely don't want any more trouble." She sniffed again, ignoring the moisture tracking down one cheek.

The cockatoo tipped his regal head to the side and continued to stare at her. Then, he jumped visibly when she burst into tears.

The look on his sisters' faces was not of amusement when they opened the door to him. They both glared fuzzily at him and groaned in unison before resignedly stepping back to allow him inside.

Yawning, Cass tightened the sash on her robe while Caro demanded, "Why are you here at this hour with an overnight bag?"

"Isn't it obvious?" her twin muttered with derision. "Meg gave him the boot. I wondered how long it would take before she wised up."

"Cass! What a terrible thing to say. Come into the living room, Steven."

Trudging past his siblings, he dropped his load and collapsed on the couch. They followed and stood at each end, surveying his dejected expression and sagging shoulders.

Caro tutted compassionately.

Cass quirked an eyebrow and wondered aloud, "He must have done something infinitely stupid. Meg doesn't strike me as the intolerant type."

"No, but she's pretty willy-nilly about him, I think." Caro went on as if he weren't in the room, "It's probably just a tiff."

"You think?"

"Mmm-hmm."

Steven's gaze shifted back to Cass as she ventured, "I guess we're stuck with him for the duration."

"Yeah. You get the blankets. I'll get the brandy."

Minutes later, they roused him from his dispirited position and made his bed while he tossed back the burning liquid that Caro had placed in his hand. Still uncommunicative, he rubbed his jaw, grunted dumbly, and they said goodnight.

She'd kicked him out.

Returning to the couch, he lifted the remote and aimed it at the TV, morosely flicking through the channels in an effort to distract himself from depressing thoughts.

On the drive over, he'd vented his anger on his car, screeching tires and slamming on brakes with unnecessary force. He couldn't believe that after all they'd meant to each other, she'd withdrawn from him so completely at her time of need. He was still raw from that biting remark about their lovemaking being only sex. Damn it, he cared! Meg must realize that.

He'd give her a day or two to collect herself. After that, the gloves were coming off.

What he wouldn't give to be able to strangle Alice and Harry right at that very moment. It boggled him that they could be so callous and uncaring, unmindful of the effect their selfishness had on Meg. He almost choked the remote because he remembered the beaten slump of her shoulders, the sad look in her eyes when she'd come home. How could they do that to her?

Absently, he clicked up and down the channels until he stopped on a National Geographic special. There on the screen, in all his salmon-crested glory, was a haughty cockatoo peering out at him.

Steven sighed. He was homesick already.

Arthur nearly had a coronary when Meg called him the next day. She was more than a little alarmed at his intensified wheezing, the old man's shortened breath sounding almost painful through the phone.

"Arthur, are you sure you're okay?"

"Dear girl, the only thing wrong with me is this absurd idea you have regarding your inheritance. I couldn't have heard right. Perhaps my senses are failing after all."

Meg cleared her throat and started over. "I want you to transfer all of it over to them, Arthur. As soon as possible. The money, the stocks and bonds, the estate — everything."

"Megan . . ." he began in a pleading tone, but she cut him off.

"I've never wanted any of it, you know that."

"Yes, but to hand it all over to those two undeserving con artists . . . Why, it's — it's like rewarding them for everything they didn't do." Only slightly composed now, Arthur reminded her, "Niles would roll over in his grave. He wanted you to pass on the family name, his legacy."

"If I ever have the lapse of common sense it takes to get married, the first thing I'll do is get rid of the Layton name," Meg bitterly informed him. "As for Niles' legacy, it's always been tainted, hasn't it?"

"Not always, dear. Niles was a good man once. It was the memory of him as a younger man that kept me loyal to him all those years. I kept hoping he'd revert, mellow out, but he never did. Money does have a strange effect on some people."

"Arthur, the money just keeps growing, the house is sitting unused. I'll never touch it." She softened her tone, picturing the aging lawyer at his desk, frowning at the wall. "You don't have any need for it, do you? I mean, if you're depending on an income from the estate, I can—"

"No, no, no." Arthur chuckled dryly. "You're sweet to be concerned for an old geezer, but I made my fortune—quite legally, I might add—after Niles passed away. I'm well taken care of."

"Good. Then you shouldn't mind escaping the albatross that is his estate. Let Alice and Harry have it." *And good riddance.*

"Are you sure?"

"Absolutely."

Arthur murmured, "I still don't think they ought to be given so much for so little, Megan. They were abominable guardians."

"From what I hear, they may have to turn the bulk of it over to several tax agencies around the globe and a handful of banks. They are also abominable bookkeepers."

The phone rang several times throughout the day, but Meg let it go to voice mail and embarked on a cleaning binge, scouring every surface and cubbyhole in the apartment. All except the spare room that still held most of Steven's things. There, she stopped at the threshold, furniture polish and rag in hand, and glumly decided to just keep the door closed. No wrinkled jeans at the foot of his bed would make her feel guilty. No dent in the pillow where last he'd slept would compel her to call him.

She dusted the living room with jerky movements, paying no heed to the lumpy *paperweight* and *candy dish* sitting forlornly on the coffee table. But eventually, the misshapen ornaments were stashed beneath the sofa cushions—out of sight if not out of mind. She'd have to remember not to sit on them.

With nothing left to clean, she gave in to curiosity and

played back the messages on her machine.

Alice had called to enquire if the *arrangements* were going smoothly.

Jonas growled at her to put his partner out of his misery — and therefore, Jonas out of his.

Caro cheerfully informed her that one night of her brother on their couch and tearing up the kitchen while attempting to make breakfast was more than she could handle. Cass agreed — loudly for once — from the background.

Olaf wanted to be sure she'd made it home all right and invited her and Steven over for a party at Fannie's.

Finally, Steven's voice said rather calmly, "Don't forget to water the bird. I know how you are when you're working."

She played that message six times.

Alice called again, so she erased the lot of them in agitation.

"Not even twenty-four hours he's gone," Meg remarked to Baz, "and everyone seems intent on reminding me that he lived here for a couple of weeks. Well, he didn't *live* here, he just *visited*. He wasn't supposed to stay. No one ever does."

Baz stepped across the table where she sat, carefully moving closer to look up at her in bewilderment.

"I know. You're still here." She rubbed his puffy chest affectionately. "But you're no sexy, six-foot-plus of grinning Kincaid. My own fault, I guess. Now it's just me and a stuck-up bird."

Offended, the conceited creature dropped to the floor and headed for his newspaper.

"I don't care how grumpy you get either. I'm not calling him. It's better he leave now than later." *It was*, she repeated silently, though the notion rang hollow in her heart.

Baking had served as useful distraction in the past, so she set about gathering the ingredients for chocolate chip cookies. She managed to concentrate long enough to get one tray out of the oven and another one in. Watching them cool on the counter for a full ten minutes, she exhaled noisily and slid them onto a plate.

The knock jarred her out of another trance, and she looked to the door, expecting to see Steven on the other side of the glass. Instead, a sandy-haired mop popped up as Johnny banged again.

Meg couldn't help but smile a little when she opened the door. He grinned gapingly and held out a bag for her inspection.

"Wanna buy a bar?"

"What kind? And who are you selling them for?" she distrustfully asked. It wouldn't be a stretch to imagine Johnny lifting the goodies from a store and peddling them for himself.

"Our basketball team. We're goin' on a tournament." He peeked over her shoulder. "Is Mr. Kinket here? He promised to go wiff us."

Meg swallowed. "He's not here right now."

"Oh. When will he be home?"

Home. She battled the sting in her eyes and motioned Johnny inside. "I'm not sure."

"Whatcha cookin'?" He furtively leaned toward the counter and sniffed. "Smells good."

"You like chocolate chip? They're still warm," Meg offered.

Almost shyly, he nodded.

Half an hour later, they'd both polished off the plate of cookies, two glasses of milk, and a bar each. Meg bought the rest and saw a very contented Johnny off again. He was a nice kid, she considered, when he wasn't trying to commit criminal acts or desecrating the front lawn.

Chapter Ten

The calls from Steven's family members and Meg's friends
stopped after two days. Then the visits began.

Viv Mackenzie *popped* in and persuaded her to go to lunch
on Wednesday. Although Meg initially refused, citing chores
as the main excuse, she gave in when the glowing pregnant
woman looked pointedly around the shining kitchen and
said, "Goodness, Meg, it doesn't need another coat of wax
right now!"

They went to a café, exchanging small talk and avoiding
the subject of Steven by tacit agreement.

Feeling more comfortable than she expected, Meg relaxed
and enjoyed the sunshine on the walk back.

"I don't mean to pry," Viv spoke up as they sat in the living room for one last cup of decaf coffee, "but is everything
okay with you and your parents?"

A bit startled at the abrupt change of topic, Meg carefully
put her mug aside. "My parents and I don't have what you'd
call a typical relationship."

"I don't want you to think Steven's been talking out of
turn or anything, but he's concerned."

Meg nodded and was quiet for a moment, choosing her
words guardedly. "Steven is used to a completely different
family life than I am. I don't think I'm cut out for marriage
and kids. Heck, I wouldn't have the first clue about any of
it." She folded her hands in her lap and watched the movement with more attention than it warranted. "I have no intention of letting Steven believe otherwise, as much as he

wants to. He'd be sorely disappointed."

Viv squeezed her arm in understanding. "I don't think so." She chuckled softly. "The Kincaid clan was sizing you up at the barbecue. We all thought you were a hit with the kids—and it doesn't take a brain surgeon to see how much you care for Steven."

"That's beside the point, isn't it?" Meg asked unhappily. "He needs someone who can be a good mother. Look at the example I have to follow. Alice's idea of parenting is remembering to even mention she has a daughter, not *show up* for dance recital or graduation."

"Whew! That bad?"

Meg snorted. "That's the least of it."

"All the same," Viv gently put forward, "I don't believe it's genetic."

"But still—"

"Do you love him?"

Stunned by the bold question, Meg could only stare blankly at her. "We haven't known each other long enough."

"Posh. I think I've loved Jonas since the first time I stumbled on him." Her eyes had a faraway look in them before she seemed to snap back to the present. "Well?"

"What?" Meg prevaricated.

"Do . . . you . . . love . . . Steven?"

"Of course, but I'd prefer you didn't tell him that."

"Suits me." Viv shrugged and pushed her swollen self up off the couch. "That's your job anyway."

No sooner had one relative of Steven's left when two more dropped in for coffee. Coffeed out herself, she perked some in the hot pink machine for the twins and settled at the kitchen table for another personal onslaught. Oddly, she found she didn't mind their interest as she might have a few short weeks ago. That was how the Kincaids operated. They looked out for one another.

"You have to take him back." Caro leveled a severe glare across the table. "He's driving us insane. One more cockatoo video, and I'll scream. Where is this Bazil character anyhow?" She craned her neck, searching beyond Meg for the bird.

"Baz is in Steven's room — I mean, the spare room."

"Ah." Caro winked at her sister. "I guess he misses him."

Cass arched a fine eyebrow and sipped her coffee.

Red as a beet, Meg remarked stiffly, "He's spoiled. He has to learn that he can't always have everything he wants."

"Hmm. That's a problem us humans have. For instance, you want our brother — even if you won't admit it — and we want peace and quiet. With one simple, amicable switch, we'd all be happy." She nudged Cass and smiled brilliantly.

Groaning, Meg shook her head. "It's complicated."

"No, it isn't. Cass and I can drive him home."

"That's not what I meant."

Caro sighed. "Damn. We know you have some things to sort out, but if I catch him burning eggs again he's . . ." She cast about helplessly, then sputtered, "*toast!* And he finds a way to char that, too."

"He does," Cass affirmed lowly.

"Oh! He sent this." Caro pulled a piece of paper from her jeans pocket and handed it over.

Meg's lips quirked slightly as she read the bold script. "I want visitation with the bird. Be home at eight. Please. Steven."

That evening, she checked her appearance for the third time, assuring herself she had *not* dressed to impress him. The short floral shift wasn't really new — she'd tried it on. Her hair had *needed* to be washed and brushed until it shone, falling carelessly upon her shoulders — just the way he liked. The light perfume she wore was *her* favorite — if he'd commented it drove him crazy she didn't recall.

If cockatoos could smirk, then smirk he did. Meg knew if she couldn't fool a bird, she may as well give up trying to fool herself.

Butterflies took flight in her stomach when his car pulled in, and she smoothed damp palms down her hips as she went to the door.

Steven was clad in pleated khaki pants and an open-neck cotton shirt. She pretended not to notice the scent of his cologne when he halted a mere hair's-breadth away, green gaze roaming her face hungrily.

"Miss me, Meggie?" he rumbled.

Stepping back, she waved him inside, being careful to keep a safe distance between them. The way her heart was pounding at the sight of him told her that anything else wouldn't be prudent.

"Baz is in the living room."

"You didn't answer me."

She folded her arms defensively. "It's quieter."

"You do miss me." He lifted a strand of her hair and rubbed it against his mouth.

"I like the silence. It was that way before." She yanked her hair away, apprehensive with the way her breathing had altered.

"Before what?" he silkily enquired. "Before I became your roommate? Your lover?" Crowding her against the wall, he continued in a guttural tone. "Do you miss the sound of us in bed, Meg? The way I whispered what I wanted and what I wanted to do to you?"

She prayed for the uncontrollable trembling in her limbs to stop, knowing full well she'd given herself away.

Steven laughed gently and dipped his head. Just as she thought he would kiss her lips, he veered to the left and brushed her cheek. Then he was gone.

Tease. He'd sensed she wanted him to kiss her and left her cold . . . again.

She made herself busy for the next twenty minutes as he conversed with Baz in the other room. She stayed out of his way, making coffee and wiping down the counter awkwardly for the hundredth time. Really, she had to stop cleaning the apartment and get some work done, she pondered.

Meg jumped when he cleared his throat from behind her, not having heard him enter over the running water. "You can take him for tonight if you want. Just have him back before nine. I'm bringing him to the vet for a checkup."

"He seems okay."

"It's only routine. We probably should have taken him when we got him."

"Hmm."

It felt as if his eyes were burning a hole in her back. "Do you want to get some more clothes?"

"Nope."

"You may as well," she said nervously.

Steering her away from the subject of moving his things, he probed, "How are your parents?"

"Fine."

"No one showed up at the hotel with an arrest warrant yet?"

"Ha, ha. Funny." She tossed the dishcloth over the faucet and turned around. Lifting her chin, she announced, "I'm giving them the estate and everything that goes with it."

Steven only nodded slowly. "I figured you might."

"Aren't you going to tell me I'm nuts?" She'd expected a bigger reaction than she was getting.

"It's one of the reasons you're so unhappy. Why not get rid of it?"

"I'm not unhappy."

He rubbed his neck tiredly and grinned. "Well, not all the time. At least, not when I was here."

Meg looked away from his heated gaze, quashing the automatic response in the pit of her stomach.

"Maybe once you've dumped the inheritance you can let go of the rest, Meg."

"Meaning?"

"You know exactly what I mean." Moving closer, he lowered his mouth to hers and gave her what she'd wanted — needed — all along. "You know where I am."

As she watched him go, she wondered if she was capable of freeing herself from the bad memories and pain of her childhood. She admitted that she *had* been unhappy, discontent on a deeply personal level before he'd come into her life. The joy she'd experienced from simply being in his company was a foreign thing to her. Perhaps that was why she distrusted it so.

She trusted Steven. Maybe the rest would follow.

The next morning, she took Baz for his checkup. The vet was kind and extremely solicitous toward him, but he squawked in protest at being handled. Given a clean bill of health, he was back to his old self by the time she got him home.

Her next errand took much longer than anticipated. After finding Arthur Muldoon's Victorian house, she was left to twiddle her thumbs in the den for half an hour before the attorney materialized. Full of apology, he barreled in on a cane and shut the door with some force.

"Dratted woman," he muttered. "She's a fine cook and housekeeper, but her memory is deplorable. Neglected to mention you were here 'til I told her I was expecting someone." He shook Meg's hand warmly and led her to a chair. "You're looking lovely, as always, dear girl."

"You seem to be doing fine, as well." She waited for him to be seated behind his desk and added, "I'm sorry we have to meet over all this business. It's been a long time since I've seen you."

"Indeed it has. Can't say as I blame you, though." His weathered face crooked in a smile. "I imagine you've put anyone and anything that reminds you of that cursed house behind you."

Meg shrugged, thinking how far off the mark that statement was.

"Well, let's get this over with." Pulling open a drawer, Arthur lifted a thick folder and placed it on his blotter. "Here is the paperwork I've been able to complete thus far. The contents of the bank accounts are all ready to be signed over. I just need your signature here," he tapped a gnarled finger on a form, "and here."

Several minutes passed while they took care of the necessary documents to transfer all of Niles Layton's liquid assets to his daughter and former son-in-law. During that time, the housekeeper brought tea and cakes, and Arthur encouraged Meg to have a few bites. He was very thorough with the paperwork, his mind as sharp as she remembered. Every now and then, he asked about her career and personal interests. He listened avidly, reminding her also that he'd been a people person, intrigued by those around him.

Prompted by this last thought, she decided to delve into his store of information. "Arthur, can you tell me why my grandfather left me most of his holdings instead of Alice? Wouldn't the natural thing be to leave it to his only offspring?"

Settling more comfortably in his leather chair, he slipped off his glasses and stuck the ear piece in his mouth. Chewing on it was an old habit she had witnessed countless times. "Niles was a difficult man to understand. If you crossed him, he never forgot it. Not even the follies of youth could be excused in his mind. Alice was flighty, given to trouble that he was constantly getting her out of."

"Trouble?"

"Mmm. Nothing too serious, you understand, just very embarrassing to him."

Somehow, this revelation did not surprise Meg in the least. Alice still did embarrassing things. Well, to her daughter they were. Like scamming money from people and ringing up debts that rivaled the national deficit of a third world country.

"Alice doesn't mind a bit of scandal, but surely he wouldn't cut her off for it? Arthur?" she nudged when he averted his eyes.

Evasively, he said, "I shouldn't discuss such things."

"Is it covered under attorney-client privilege?"

"No, but . . ." He exhaled gustily. "He didn't cut her off. I mean, you know he left a fair sum of money to your mother. It was not what she expected, even if he did make a point of telling her the contents of his will. Alice didn't believe that out of such a vast fortune he would only pass on what she considered a pittance to her and Harry—but he did."

Curiosity kept Meg silent as he seemed to consider how much to divulge.

"One time, Alice crashed into a car while driving drunk. No one was injured, miraculously, but she was charged with it. It was all over the papers. Niles was apoplectic."

"I don't recall that."

"Before your time, dear. Alice was still a teenager."

"He limited her inheritance as punishment?"

Arthur shook his gray head. "No. She got off on a technicality. The police officer neglected to read her her rights upon arrest. Still, the public humiliation angered Niles."

"Then why . . ." Confused, Meg let the question hang between them.

"The final straw came when Alice was caught *in flagrante* with a front-running politician for the premier's office. *That* caused the second biggest blow-up of all. Of course, your mother laughed it off, delighted with all the notoriety." He tutted in an old-fashioned manner. "The worst situation Alice created didn't hit the news, only because Niles threatened not to leave her a single penny. She was gung-ho for a very public custody battle with Fred—" He caught himself guiltily, a red flush flooding his wrinkled cheeks.

The implications of that unguarded comment struck Meg with the force of a sledgehammer. "Custody battle? Alice had a child for Dr. Reynolds?"

"Oh my." Arthur retrieved a hankie from his pocket and mopped the beads of sweat from his brow.

Dry-mouthed, she demanded, "Do I have a sibling I don't know about?"

"Heavens, my big mouth! This is one can of worms best left unopened."

"*Arthur!*" The prospect of having a brother or sister out there had a strange effect on Meg. The idea was not entirely unwelcome, though being kept in the dark had her seeing red. "I deserve to know. Do I have a sibling?"

"No, no. It's a long story, Megan. Perhaps you ought to discuss this with your mother."

"Do you think Alice will be straight with me?" she queried dryly.

Arthur drew a deep breath and contemplated her for a moment. "Certainly not. It doesn't reflect well on her."

"Then tell me," she pleaded, sensing the information he imparted could change her life.

"Alice began seeing Fred Reynolds the year before you were born. Niles didn't approve. He expected her to marry into a family as wealthy as his own. This was mainly why Alice continued to see him. You see, back then Fred was not established as one of the best in his field. He was relatively young, still idealistic." Arthur smiled in remembrance. "He was a fine young man—too trusting for Alice's maneuvers."

"What happened?"

"Well, your mother came to Niles one day and told him she was four months pregnant."

"With Fred's child?" Bafflement colored Meg's voice. If they'd begun seeing each other in the year before she was born . . . then that would make the doctor her father.

"I know what you're thinking, but let me finish. It's not as cut and dried as that." He waited until he had her full attention once more. "Alice knew it was too late for—well, an abortion—so, she expected that Niles would hand over a hefty chunk of money to her and Fred for the child. Fred, by the way, was totally in the dark about her plan. He'd signed up for a stint as a volunteer in Africa and assumed Alice would marry him and go as well. He was thrilled with the prospect of impending fatherhood and wanted to have the wedding as soon as possible.

"Alice was not enticed by the lure of Africa at all. For the next three months, however, she let Fred believe she was. It bought her the time she needed to work on Niles. Since he was livid, as expected, she had to come up with an alternate strategy. Going away with Fred was not an option for her. She didn't even wish to be married to the man, no matter how bright his future."

"Then why date him to start with?" The depth of her mother's conniving was becoming clear, so clear that she answered her own question. "She knew Niles wanted something different."

Arthur nodded solemnly. "And she wasn't above blackmail to get what she wanted out of him."

"Are you saying she got pregnant on purpose?"

"I suspect so. I think she grew tired of having a set allowance. The more money she spent, the more she wanted. Caring for a future heir would have practically guaranteed a lump sum of money. Niles was, after all, preoccupied with carrying on the Layton legacy. He would have done just about anything to ensure the child stayed under his roof and bore his name."

"Was I that child?"

"Yes."

Meg leaned back in her chair, eyes closed. "The circumstances surrounding my conception are a little hard for me to digest, Arthur. I never dreamed Alice could be *that* duplicitous." She massaged her aching temples. "I still don't understand about Fred Reynolds."

"Alice—while having no intention of carrying out the threat—swore to Niles that she would marry Fred and head for Africa. Niles countered with an offer of a great deal of money if she didn't. Alice got what she wanted.

"She then went to Fred and confessed she'd been unfaithful. The whole time she was seeing him . . . she was seeing another man. Their courtship was only a ruse, she told him, to provoke Niles into giving in."

Her mother's cruelty knew no bounds. How could she behave so badly toward a man as sweet as the doctor? Remembering the first meeting with him, she realized how awful it must have been to come face to face with that horrible chapter in his past. Not only that, but to look the woman who might have been his daughter right in the eye.

Arthur brought her out of her reverie by clearing his throat. "Fred was devastated. He demanded a blood test as soon as Alice delivered, vowed to sue for custody."

"But it was negative . . . and the man she was secretly involved with was Harry?"

"Yes. A distantly related Layton whom Niles would have had no problem with her marrying—and didn't. Heartbroken, Fred went off to Africa. I heard he met and married a lovely girl there. The rest, as they say, is history." With that,

Arthur shrugged fatalistically and folded his hands. "It hardly matters now."

Meg wasn't so sure. Before she left, one more question had to be dealt with. "The paternity test, Arthur, who performed it?"

"Why, Niles' own physician, if I remember correctly. He's dead now, too, poor soul."

"Do you think he might have been persuaded to tamper with the results?" The reason the doctor had seemed so familiar to Meg crystallized in one profound moment of lucidity. She pictured his face that first time at the Mackenzie's, the faded blue eyes so like her own . . . and she knew that Alice had committed the ultimate act of treachery against her daughter.

The sun was setting on a humid day as Steven waited on the steps for her. He was worried again. It seemed like he did a lot of that lately, but Meg was someone he didn't mind fretting over. Hell, judging by the call he'd gotten from Fred, she deserved fretting over. She must be upset.

Replaying the conversation with the doctor, he clenched his teeth. The man had rung from the hotel lobby to warn him that Meg had overheard an argument between him and Alice. Without getting into details, he said that some pretty ugly things were bandied about, and she had stormed off. Steven hadn't demanded to know what Fred's part in the whole mess was, but it was clear that he was also disturbed.

Luckily, he'd been able to catch the call. Fred probably wasn't aware that he was no longer staying with Meg. He'd fabricate any excuse to be in the apartment when she got back. The truth was, he'd decided to beg if he had to. He wanted back into her home, her life.

Plus, he'd forgotten how rotten it was to cohabit with siblings of the female persuasion.

When her car pulled in, he stood and waited for her to reach the steps.

"You shouldn't let Baz wander out." She indicated the open door to the apartment. "I'm not in the mood to chase him."

"I can see that. He's in the living room with a National Geographic video. I think he needs a mate. He almost jumped through the screen when the cockatoos came on." Slipping a hand beneath the fall of her hair, he was gratified when she didn't move away. "Do you mind that I'm here?"

"No. I'm glad. It's been a terrible, terrible day." She went willingly into his embrace and stayed there until he scooped her up and took her inside.

"Fred called," he told her while they went down the hall.

"How much did he tell you?"

"Just that there had been a scene. Want to talk about it?"

"Later. Right now I want a hot shower and my fuzzy robe." She slid to the floor in front of the bathroom and kissed his cheek. "I really am glad you're here."

"I'll be in the kitchen making dinner. *Sandwiches*," he affirmed when she cut him a severe look. "I do know my limitations."

"That's not what your sisters told me."

"I needed a diversion. I was miserable."

"I'm sorry," she whispered.

"You'll make it up to me."

Hours later they sprawled on the couch, and Steven tried to figure out how best to ease into the discussion. He'd avoided any mention of Fred, her family, or the inheritance during supper. Meg was obviously feeling raw emotionally, and he didn't want to bring up what happened today before she was ready.

He was still at a loss, trying to understand Fred's place in the scheme of things when she blurted, "He's my father . . . I think."

"What?"

"You must be wondering what the connection is, why Fred would be arguing with Alice and why hearing it would upset me." She told him about her visit with Niles' attorney and how she'd put the pieces together before confronting her mother. Fred had had his suspicions and was already there, grilling her about the validity of the paternity test outside the suite. Meg had eavesdropped unashamedly, knowing she wouldn't get a direct response out of Alice. But her mother had admitted the deception to her former lover, laughing in an almost lighthearted way before noticing Meg's presence in the hall. She'd gone white then, stammering that she was only joking.

"She wasn't, though," Meg murmured dully. "She was just frightened that I'd change my mind about helping her out of financial trouble."

"Did you?"

"Hardly. I gave her the papers with the stipulation that neither she nor Harry ever contact me again."

Steven hugged her, consoling her with a gentle kiss on the forehead. "Was it difficult?"

She sighed and snuggled closer. "Not really. I'd decided to tell her that anyway. Alice wouldn't have shown up with Harry in tow if not for the money. She couldn't get it without going through me. I could see she just wanted to take the lot of it and run. I'm not even as hurt as I'd expected. I suppose I should be. Honestly, I'm more angry that she lied about who my father really was — *is*."

"How do you feel about that?"

"I don't know. I didn't stick around to ask him how *he* felt."

"He sounded pretty shaken up when I spoke with him,

Meg." Cautiously, he suggested, "Maybe you should call him yourself."

"Not now. It's all so strange. I mean, all my life I thought Harry was my father. To know that it's someone else will take some getting used to."

A crash in the kitchen had them bolting upright. They rushed to the other room and discovered the bird cage on the floor and an innocent-looking Baz strutting across the table.

"You know," Meg ventured, "I think you're right. He does need a mate."

"Uh-huh. He's suffering from severe boredom."

"I'll go to the pet shop in the morning."

"I'll go with you." Steven stooped and picked up the battered cage. "We're going to need something bigger." Realizing that implied they share the second bird, he added, "Unless you think I should keep one at my place. They could visit."

She studied her nails in fascination. "Well, why don't we see how it goes? If you don't mind staying the night, that is."

Wrapping his arms around her, he declared, "Whatever you want."

"I want you to hold me."

So he did. All night he held her intimately, but they didn't have sex. Limbs entwined, they slept so soundly that the alarm couldn't rouse them for a full five minutes. In the middle of the sixth, she slapped the snooze button and shoved him out of bed.

Face up on the floor, he grinned. "My God, it's good to be home!"

The next day, Meg went to Rosa's restaurant with some trepidation. She was shown to a table with a lone occupant. As the distinguished man stood gracefully, she recognized that he was equally nervous.

"Dr. Reynolds." Conscious of her shaking hand, she stuck it out anyway. It was accepted in a firm grip and held on to for a few seconds as he searched her face. "Thank you for seeing me."

"That isn't necessary. I was happy to hear from you. I didn't know if I would. At least, not this soon."

They ordered and sat in stiff silence, neither knowing quite how to begin. Finally, Fred cleared his throat.

"Even though it's redundant at this point, I assume you want another blood test." He fiddled with his soup spoon and then purposefully laid it aside. "I want you to know that if I had known you were mine, I would never have gone away."

Meg dipped her head in acknowledgment, having accepted the fact that he'd tried to claim parentage. "I know. Alice did a number on both of us. I'm not certain where to go from here."

"I was hoping we could try to develop some kind of relationship."

She smiled a little. "I guess we could get to know one another." A longing she had yet to satisfy came hot on the heels of that statement. Was it too much to hope that this gentle man was sincere? "I know you didn't expect to become a father—"

"On the contrary," he interrupted quietly, "I once looked forward to that very thing. I wanted very much to be your father, Meg. I still do. If Alice hadn't sent me packing . . . well, that was a mixed blessing, I guess. I wouldn't have met my wife if she hadn't."

"Were you married long?"

"Over twenty years. She died a while back. My only regret was that we couldn't have children." He covered her hand with his. "Which is another reason why you are a welcome surprise to me. Will we do some catching up?"

Meg grasped her father's hand and smiled tremulously. In a watery voice, she said, "I'd like that."

"Are you going to marry me or not?" Steven growled in her ear. His breathing hadn't returned to normal from their lovemaking, his depleted body still joined with hers.

Meg skimmed her hands over his sweat-slickened back sensuously. "I'm thinking it over."

Weeks had passed since her meeting with Fred, and they'd spent a good deal of time together. She was sure her artistic gene had come from him as she'd seen several of his own works. He denied having any real talent, but his *dabbles* were pleasing to the eye. She liked him as a person, was happy to have found out about him when she had.

Alice and Harry had moved to Layton House as the clause in Niles' will did not restrict it from being *given* away. They had been found by Scotland Yard and Interpol, however. Arthur told her they'd be in court for a while, no doubt spending a large portion of their windfall in litigation.

The Kincaids were treating her like one of the family, as if she hadn't kicked the favorite son out of her home. The twins were most grateful and had sent her a dozen yellow roses the day after she'd let him back in.

Baz had a female companion they'd named Gladys because he'd sure seemed glad to make her acquaintance. Now they wondered how long it would be until those three eggs hatched and who would adopt them.

Johnny blew in regularly, alternately driving Steven mad and tickling his funny bone. He'd learned to appreciate the kid's quirky side and was wholeheartedly committed to the upcoming basketball tournament.

As patient and empathetic as Steven had proved to be, it was apparent he was nearing the end of his rope. She knew it was difficult for him considering one of his most infuriating qualities was being bullheaded.

"How do you like ultimatums?" he mumbled to the side of her neck.

"I don't." She giggled when he pinched her bottom.

"Love me?"

"You know I do."

"You've yet to say it."

Soberly, Meg whispered, "I love you."

Lifting his head, he kissed her for a long time. "Say it again." His body was getting harder inside her.

"I love you, Steven." She urged him to move faster and relished the feel of his climax as she repeated the words over and over. "I'd love to marry you."

Before slipping into an exhausted sleep, he told her, "I knew you'd come to your senses eventually."

Meg only laughed, thinking it was a good thing he was so pushy!

YOU MAY ALSO ENJOY THE FOLLOWING FROM EXTASY BOOKS INC:

What JJ Wants
Quinn Clancy and Mary Clancy

Excerpt

Weddings always had this effect on her. Just the simple act of watching two people so devoted to each other created an illusion of serenity in her own jumbled life. Problems seemed insignificant for a little while, and she got caught up in the moment. There were no resumes to mail, no bills to pay, no worries whatsoever.

Apparently, the sight of matrimonial bliss did not affect JJ Vanzant the same way. She'd gotten a glimpse of him practically hidden behind a darkened fern, staring into his glass with a too-somber expression on his face. His broad shoulders had risen and fallen slowly, as if resettling an invisible burden. For long minutes she'd watched before her feet made the decision to walk over to him.

Now, as one big hand rested in the small of her back and the other cradled hers against his chest, she wondered if giving in to the urge to wipe that troubled look away had been wise. His cologne mingled with another, more elusive scent that she knew was distinctly his—a bit spicy and very sensual. Without thinking, she edged closer, the top of her head brushing his chin. He leaned down and pressed his cheek to hers, and she knew she ought to back off. After all, she'd spent the entire evening trying to stay out of his way, so this was definitely sending the wrong signal. She considered putting some distance between his slightly rougher cheek and hers, but her traitorous face would not cooperate. This really wasn't wise.

JJ was careful of her, his touch almost tender as they swayed to the love song being played by the string quartet. Alex fancied he was very respectful of her smaller, less substantial frame. Skinny, she ruefully corrected. She'd lost a lot of weight while she'd been ill and hadn't gained much of it back. Her wrists were too thin, and her ribs were too prominent to anyone with a mind to examine them. Thankfully, no one had.

She closed her drooping lids and sighed. Who was she kidding anyway? A whiff of the man was all she could afford with so much on her plate—and JJ was way out of her league. No handsome, successful, fun-loving guy in his right mind would take on a relationship with someone who carried a load as big as hers. Certainly not one who, by his own earlier admission, was commitment-shy.

"Song's over." JJ's arms remained around her. "Want another, or is one dance all you can stomach with me?"

"I don't mind one more—but I'll probably fall asleep on you."

He laughed softly and tucked her head under his chin. "I'll chance it."

So they stayed that way until Steven Kincaid asked to cut in. The glare JJ sent him was ignored with a grin, and he glided with Alex across the floor.

The reception lasted almost 'til midnight, everyone waltzing with everyone else. Finally, the long-awaited moment for the tossing of the bouquet and garter arrived.

Alex was dragged into the laughing group of single

women, stunned when the bride threw the rose blooms directly at her. It thunked on her chest, and she automatically put her hands up to save the lovely creation from crashing to the floor. The other guests roared in appreciation and shouted for the groom to get rid of the scrap of something blue in his hand, and her face burned.

Jonas flipped the garter over his shoulder in the opposite direction of where the bachelors had gathered, seemingly oblivious to the fact that JJ had deliberately held himself apart from the rest. The blond man was startled to find the lacy thing on his head and grinned sassily as he plucked it from its resting place.

Grateful that she was wearing pants, Alex complied with tradition, and she extended her leg for JJ to do the honors. The suit was fashionably loose, however, which enabled him to slide the fabric above her knee. And was it just her imagination, or did those warm hands linger unnecessarily on her bare skin?

Disregarding her flaming embarrassment, he rose and gallantly brought her hand to his lips, blue gaze burning into hers amid more cheers. She scowled back, not comfortable at all with the predatory gleam there.

"Lighten up, Alex. I don't bite." He smiled down at her and added, "Well, not very hard and only in private." Wiggling thick eyebrows, he leered comically.

"Forget it, Romeo," she told him, "I'm not your flavour."

"I'm all for trying new things."

"I'm not," Alex said truthfully and turned away from his wicked grin.

But he wasn't finished. "Can I offer you a lift home?"

"I have a ride, thank you. Cass and Caro are staying at Viv's house, just up the street." She hurried out into the hall where guests were saying goodnight to the couple. They would spend the night in their home and depart for a short honeymoon in the morning, Eleuthera having tactfully checked herself and the out-of-town guests into a hotel to give them privacy.

Alex hugged the newlyweds warmly and went to find her coat, only to have it placed around her shoulders by JJ. She muttered a stiff "Thanks" and searched for the twins. Desperately, she tried to pretend Mr. Dimples wasn't right on her heels.

"We've decided to go to the hotel for a little post-party party. Everyone's invited," Caro told her. "Or we can drop you off first if you're tired."

"I am tired," Alex said, unable to hide a yawn, "but I'll get a cab."

"Nonsense," interjected the aggravating man behind her. "I can drop you." He slipped an arm around her and grinned affably. "I know the way."

That was it. She was boxed in. Smiling as brightly as she could, she let him lead her off.

"I don't know what it is about me that offends you," he groused as he fired up the sporty jeep. "I mean, an invitation to supper or a movie hardly sounds like an insult."

Alex kept her attention on the passing scenery.

"I'm an easy-going guy. I have all my own hair and teeth." He tapped his fingers impatiently on the wheel. "I'm self-supporting . . . kind to animals."

There was a loose thread on her pants. She plucked it off.

"I give to local charities and international child relief on a regular basis."

She coughed.

"My socks match. Usually. Did I say that already?"

"What does it stand for?" she asked curiously.

Thrown at the change of subject, he looked askance. "What?"

"Your initials. Is it John Jacob or Julian Joseph or —"

"It's J-A-Y J-A-Y," he spelled.

"You're lying."

Blushing, he growled, "My mother had a twisted sense of humor. Let it go."

Flicking him a glance, she pointed out, "You're going the wrong way."

"No, I'm just taking a more relaxing route." There was a full minute of silence. "How about we go to a movie sometime?"

"I can't."

"Why not?"

"Too many things to do. Responsibilities. Some of us do have them."

"I'm responsible," he replied, sounding aggrieved.

"Then you'll understand if I have to say no, thank you."

"What responsibilities can one have that don't allow for a night out every now and then?"

"How about elderly parents and two rambunctious sons who are extremely hard to find sitters for?" Not to mention expensive to find sitters for.

JJ's head whipped around at that. "You have kids?"

"The light is red," she shouted.

He slammed on the brakes, which gave them both a good jolt.

"Sorry," he said. Oddly disappointed at the notion of his being put off by the idea of children, Alex was surprised when he suggested a few minutes later, "I like kids. We could take them to a movie."

"Listen," she stated perversely, "I'm just not in a position right now to be dating, let alone to give Hank and Billy ideas about someone who won't stick around long."

"How can you say I won't stick around? You don't even know me," he protested in a rising voice.

"Have you ever sustained any semblance of a meaningful relationship with a member of the opposite sex?" she demanded.

"I could learn."

"Get your education elsewhere, Vanzant. I have too much going on." Alex spared him one hard look, trying not to let his shuttered expression tug on her emotions. She was being rather harsh, she conceded, but she was smart enough to recognize that she only presented a challenge to him and she dared not start thinking otherwise.

The rest of the ride was in silence, and she was in the midst of composing an apology when he pulled into her parents' driveway.

"I'm sor—"

"Forget it," he said, cutting her off. "I should have taken no for an answer the first time." Smiling a little sadly, he capitulated, "You're right, anyway. I am a bad risk. I'll wait until you're inside before I leave."

Knowing when to let well enough alone, Alex got out and tiredly trudged up the walk to the tiny white house and let herself in. The fading sound of the jeep seemed very lonely as she leaned against the closed door.

Later, after she'd checked on her sleeping boys and changed into her old pajamas, she paused before the full-length mirror in the hall. Scrutinizing her body from every angle, she told herself it was for the best that she never see JJ again. He was having a laugh at her expense, that was all.

The only thing that still made her resemble the old Alex was her lustrous, curling black hair. She fingered the strands reaching just past her thin shoulders and added her breasts to the short list. They, by some miracle, were still full and proud. Now if only the rest of her body—hell, her life—would catch up, she'd be happy.

She lay on her narrow bed in the dark and wondered what JJ had meant when he'd told her he was a bad risk. She sensed that something solitary and troubling lurked beneath those words, their meaning attached to a much deeper experience than skirt-chasing.

It was not her concern, she reminded herself. It mattered nothing if she'd experienced a twinge of remorse after turning him down so coldly. She'd likely only run into him occasionally through Viv and Jonas—and not then if she could avoid it.

ABOUT THE AUTHORS

Quinn and Mary Clancy are two sisters who have been writing romance for several years. Quinn is a published author but this is Mary's first books. Originally, the Triple Threat series was written in the late 90's and has been updated by the two for publication. Her Protector is the first book of the series.